Sam pulled the letter out and reread it for about the thirtieth time:

Dear Mr. and Mrs. Blady,

My name is Samantha Bridges. Actually, that's my adopted name. My adopted parents are Vernon and Carla Bridges, who live in Kansas. That's a state in the middle of the United States. Do you know it? I only found out recently that I am adopted. My actual mother, I have learned, is a Jewish woman in California named Susan Briarly. You know her, I think. I met Susan recently. She told me about Michael and her, and about you two. Well, I don't know any other way to say this than just to say it. I'm Susan and Michael's daughter. . . .

Sunset Stranger

CHERIE BENNETT

Sunset™
Island

SPLASH™

A BERKLEY / SPLASH BOOK

SUNSET STRANGER is an original publication of The Berkley Publishing Group. This work has never appeared before in book form.

SUNSET STRANGER

A Berkley Book / published by arrangement with General Licensing Company, Inc.

PRINTING HISTORY
Berkley edition / March 1994

A GLC BOOK

Splash and *Sunset Island* are trademarks belonging to General Licensing Company, Inc.

ISBN: 0-425-14129-2

BERKLEY®
Berkley Books are published by
The Berkley Publishing Group,
200 Madison Avenue, New York, New York 10016.
BERKLEY and the "B" design
are trademarks belonging to Berkley Publishing Corporation.

PRINTED IN THE UNITED STATES OF AMERICA

10 9 8 7 6 5 4 3 2 1

For my guy

ONE

"No way am I getting on that thing," Emma Cresswell said firmly.

"Yes way!" Sam Bridges insisted, holding her wild red curls away from her neck to cool off. "You're nineteen years old, and you're telling me you're afraid of a dinky little ride in a dinky little amusement park?"

"I wouldn't exactly describe it as 'dinky,'" Carrie Alden put in, eyeing the giant roller coaster that seemed to defy gravity.

"Well, I am embarrassed to even be your best friend. That's all I have to say," Sam told both of them huffily. "Where's your sense of adventure?"

"I'm much more adventurous on the ground than I would be up there," Emma

1

said, cocking her chin toward the top of the gleaming steel coaster.

"Pitiful," Sam decreed, shaking her head. The three best friends were spending their day off at Old Orchard Beach, an amusement park about thirty miles south of Portland, Maine. It had taken them about an hour to get there from Sunset Island, including the ferry ride. Sunset Island was the gorgeous resort island where they were spending their second straight summer working as au pairs.

"Look, nothing is going to happen," Sam assured her friends. "I offer you the Bridges guarantee."

"The Bridges guarantee?" Emma asked dubiously. "What's that?"

"Don't know," Sam admitted with a grin. "But it sure sounds good, doesn't it?"

At that moment a carload of girls on the roller coaster screamed as they came around a curve.

"Count me out, too," Carrie said with a wince.

"Geez, weenie central, here," Sam

2

scoffed, clutching a huge Kewpie doll she had won earlier playing Skee-Ball.

Emma ran her fingers through her perfect blond hair. "Sam," Emma reminded her, "you talked me into going on the Tilt-a-Whirl with you. Remember what happened."

"You didn't actually get sick, you just turned a little green," Sam observed. "Anyway, what's a little hurl between friends? Those hot dogs weren't worth digesting anyway!"

"Please, don't remind me," Emma said, holding her hand over her stomach.

"Anyway, I kept mine down no problem," Sam intoned.

"You've got a cast iron stomach," Emma reminded her.

"And you never gain any weight!" Carrie lamented. "Unlike someone in this trio."

"Please," Sam scoffed. "I'd like to borrow some of your curves . . . permanently."

"I still don't know how you do it," Carrie sighed, looking down at her own full figure, and then back over at Sam's long, tall form. "I mean, I guess it's just genetics—"

3

"Actually, I think it's all those corn dogs I ate at the Kansas State Fair when I was a kid. It alters a person's metabolic state for life."

"What's a corn dog?" Emma asked.

Sam gave her a look. "You're kidding, right?"

Emma just stared back at her friend.

"I should have known," Sam said with a sigh. "You've probably never even been to a state fair in your life. Am I right, Princess Grace?"

"You are correct, you common peasant," Emma teased good-naturedly. "Now tell me what a corn dog is."

"A hot dog on a stick deep fried in cornmeal batter," Sam explained. "Delish." She feinted to one side to avoid a group of youngsters walking by, waving puffs of neon-pink cotton candy like they were flashlights lighting their way.

"Sounds hideous," Emma commented.

"Sounds fattening," Carrie pointed out.

"Sounds fabulous!" Sam insisted.

They all looked at each other and laughed. As different as they were, it was amazing that they had ever become best friends.

We are so different from one another!
Sam thought. *But somehow, it works!*

Sam was a tall, model-thin, wild-haired redhead from a tiny town in Kansas. Her mother worked in a pharmacy and her father coached high school football. Sam was a talented dancer who had recently made a Broadway debut. She wanted nothing less than fame, fortune, and stardom. Sam attracted guys easily, but never could make up her mind about which one was right for her.

Emma was Sam's opposite. Born into one of the richest families in the country, the Cresswells of Boston, there was little she didn't have and nothing she couldn't have. Yet before she'd come to Sunset Island, she felt as if she hadn't even begun to figure out who she really was or what she really wanted. On the island, she'd formed her first genuine friendships, and found her first true love. Sam was often jealous of Emma's petite, blond, gorgeous looks, and her money.

And then there was Carrie, the glue that held the threesome together. From a big family in suburban New Jersey, with a curvy (she thought too curvy) body and shining dark hair, she was going into her sophomore year at Yale University in the fall and wanted to be a photojournalist. Smart, practical, and a great friend, Carrie's fresh-scrubbed girl-next-door good looks were a real contrast to her best friends' more glamorous appeal.

Sam recalled how the three of them had met at the International Au Pair Convention in New York City the year before, and almost immediately became best friends. They were all lucky enough to be hired by families who spent the summer on fabulous Sunset Island, an exclusive resort island at the far reaches of Casco Bay, off the Portland, Maine coast.

And they are the best friends I've always dreamed of having, Sam realized, looking over at Carrie and Emma. *Too cool!*

"All this talking about corn dogs has got me hungry again," Sam said, not wanting to give voice to the mushy stuff she'd just been thinking. She saw a stand selling ice cream on the other side of the fairway. "Anybody want one?"

"Eat mine for me and describe it in detail," Carrie suggested with a sigh.

"I couldn't eat a thing," Emma protested.

"Well, hold up while I buy one," Sam told them, and ran over to the ice-cream stand. "Hi," she said, smiling at the teen-aged girl behind the counter. "One large chocolate and vanilla twist in a sugar cone with extra sprinkles, please," she ordered.

"Sure," the girl said. She put a cone under the soft serve machine and filled it up as she eyed Sam's outfit. "I love what you're wearing," the girl told Sam.

"Oh, this?" Sam asked, staring down at herself with surprise. "I just kind of threw it together." She had on very baggy, very short cut-off jeans, held up with a belt made of dozens of tiny plastic Elvis Presleys. Over that she had on a denim shirt covered with peace symbols, cut off under the bust. And on her feet she wore her trademark red cowboy boots.

"Well, it looks great," the girl told Sam, taking her money.

"Thanks," Sam said. She trucked back

over to her friends and smiled as she checked out their outfits. Carrie had on baggy jeans and a Save the Whales T-shirt, and her hair was in a ponytail. Emma had on perfect white cotton shorts and a sleeveless white cotton eyelet blouse. Her hair was held back with a slender white ribbon, and small pearls decorated her ears.

Yeah, we are definitely different, Sam thought to herself with a chuckle. "Anyone want a lick?" Sam asked, holding out her cone.

"Nope," Carrie said. Emma shook her head.

"So, you guys ready to go back to the roller coaster?" Sam asked.

Emma groaned. "Can't we just go play more Skee-Ball?"

"Are you kidding?" Sam replied. "The guy running it was ready to off me because I kept winning."

"It was pretty funny," Carrie agreed.

"Listen, you guys," Sam said earnestly. "Didn't you ever hear about how you're supposed to confront your fears? This will be good for both of you!"

8

"Oh, so now you're a therapist?" Carrie asked Sam with a laugh.

"Please, please, please go on it with me," Sam begged, trying a different tact. "I'll be your best friend forever."

"Won't work. You already are," Emma pointed out.

"Okay, how's this," Sam said. "I really want to go on that thing, but I'm a little nervous and I want the two of you to go with me to hold my hand."

Carrie looked at Emma. "She's relentless, you know. If we don't say yes we'll never hear the end of it."

Emma sighed. "If I go on this, do you promise not to get on my case about anything for the rest of the day and night?"

"*Moi?*" Sam asked innocently. "On your case?"

"All right, Emma's in, I'm in," Carrie said reluctantly. "I don't believe I'm agreeing to this."

"Let's go!" Sam cried. She tugged on her friends' arms, and they paid their fee at the booth at the entrance to the roller coaster.

"You sure this thing is safe?" Carrie

asked skittishly as a carload of kids whizzed by screaming at the top of their lungs.

"There hasn't been an accident at this amusement park in eight years," the guy who took their money said. "'Course, that time two kids broke their legs," he reflected.

"Gee, I feel a whole lot better now," Carrie said sarcastically.

"C'mon. Let's get on!" Sam chortled. She led the way to a car at the very front of the roller coaster train.

"Not the lead car!" Emma protested.

"I'm getting in," Sam announced. She climbed into the seat. Carrie and Emma looked at each other. Then, slowly they climbed into the lead car next to Sam.

"I'll kill you for this," Emma hissed in Sam's ear.

"You can only kill me if you live through it," Sam replied sweetly.

The girls heard a cranking noise as the cars began to climb to the top of an enormous metal hill.

"This is gonna be great!" Sam yelled.

"I hate it already!" Emma cried with trepidation, grabbing for Carrie's hand.

Their car was poised at the brink for a brief second, and then dropped off the hill like a rock over a cliff.

Carrie and Emma screamed. Sam yelled louder. Then she turned to yell something funny to her friends, but she realized they were yelling something, too. In unison.

"SAAAAAM! I HAAATE YOUUUU-UUU!"

Hmmmmm, Sam thought, *That's weird,* as she approached the front door of the house of the Jacobs family, after Carrie and Emma dropped her off. *There's no light on in the living room.*

Sam worked for the Jacobs family—actually, for Dan Jacobs, a divorced father with two fourteen-year-old identical twins named Becky and Allie, who Sam privately referred to as "the monsters."

Dan always leaves the light on in the living room, Sam thought, as she got ready to put her key in the door. *But now it's out. In fact, almost all the lights in the house are out!* Sam looked at her watch—it was only ten-thirty, and she knew Dan, who had given her the day and the evening off, was at the country club at a cocktail party that wouldn't be over until eleven. He always left the lights in the house on when he went out. It was practically a ritual with him. Sam tried to remember what he'd said the twins would be doing.

A creepy feeling came over her, and her heart raced in her chest. *Omigod. There's someone in the house. Or someone has robbed the house. Where are Becky and Allie?*

Sam looked up. A light was on in the twins' room. It was the only light in the house.

This is seriously awful, Sam thought to herself. For a second, she considered calling the police from a neighbor's house. Then she told herself she was being ridiculous, that there was probably nothing wrong. Steeling her courage up, she put the key in the front door and turned it.

"Anyone here?" Sam whispered, moving as quietly as she could.

Then she heard a voice. A young, male voice.

"Oh my God!" the voice said, "Sam's here!"

"So what?" said a girl's voice, which Sam instantly recognized as Becky Jacobs's. "It's not like we're smoking crack or anything." Then a light came on in the living room, just where Sam was standing. She looked into the now light room. On the living room couch, sitting side by side, were Becky Jacobs and Ian Templeton. Ian Templeton was the thirteen-year-old son of rock superstar Graham Perry, for whom Carrie worked.

Ian and Becky stared at Sam. Ian looked nervous and Becky looked bored.

They were necking! Sam realized, trying not to laugh. *I can't believe I busted them necking!*

"Uh," Becky said contemptuously, looking directly at Sam, "could we have a little H and G, please?"

"H and G?" Sam echoed.

"Hello and Goodbye?" Becky explained testily. "As in we want some privacy?"

"We weren't doing anything," Ian nervously hastened to explain.

"Hey, it's not illegal to kiss," Sam said with a grin.

"My mom would kill me," Ian mumbled. Sam noticed that his hair was totally messed up, and she found this hilarious.

"No, she won't," Becky said defiantly. "Because Sam isn't going to tell her. Are you?"

"Nope," Sam agreed. "Kiss away. As long as that's all you're doing," she remembered to add. *This is so weird,* Sam thought to herself. *Me, pretending to be an adult!*

"Yeah, like I'd tell you," Becky snorted.

"What about the rest of the Zits?" Ian asked Sam nervously, ignoring Becky's comment. "You won't tell them, either, will you?"

"Well, why would I—" Sam began.

"Hey, what's your problem?" Becky interrupted. "Why can't the rest of the band know?"

"Because it's uncool, that's why," Ian explained. "I mean, the Zits are professional and everything."

Ian was referring to the other members of his band, Lord Whitehead and the Zit People, a rock band that played what Ian termed "industrial music," which

14

consisted of the band members banging on hulked-out appliances with iron pipes and singing along to prerecorded cassettes. The Jacobs twins had recently joined the band as backup singers, and Becky and Ian had become something of a young teen item.

"We'll just keep this between the three of us," Sam promised. Then she remembered a scene from her own early teen years—when she'd spent hours kissing a guy, and the next day he'd pretended he didn't even know her, and how hurt she'd been. "Just remember to be nice to each other, okay?" Sam added.

"Yeah, sure," Ian agreed.

He has no idea what I'm talking about, Sam realized. *God, do I feel old.* "Where's your sister?" she asked Becky.

"Upstairs," Becky reported. "Reading something by Ayn Rand. She's weird."

"Your parents know you're here?" Sam asked, turning to Ian.

"Yup," Ian reported. "Dad's getting me at eleven. Is that soon?"

"Pretty soon," Sam reported. "Well, I'll just leave you two be, then. See you." Sam clicked off the light switch, leaving

Ian and Becky together in the dark again.

"Thanks, Sam," Ian said.

"Ssssh!" Becky whispered. "Don't be so nice to her. She'll think we like her."

"I do like her!"

"Sssssh!"

Sam, who heard this last exchange, did everything she could to stop herself from laughing.

I am so glad I'm not fourteen anymore! she thought to herself.

About an hour later, Sam lay in bed, thinking about guys.

"Maybe being fourteen isn't so bad at that," she mumbled out loud to herself. She punched her pillow and folded it into a more comfortable position, then resumed her reverie about the dismal state of the guys in her life.

Okay, I broke up with Pres—or should I say he broke up with me? she thought to herself. Presley Travis was the cute, cool, southern guy who played bass for the popular island rock band Flirting With Danger. He and Sam had an on-again, off-again romance. But when Sam had been unwilling—or unable—to make a commitment to him, he'd broken up with her for good. Then when she wanted to get him back, she couldn't!

And then there's Danny, Sam thought. *I definitely love Danny. But in what way do I love Danny?*

Sam had met Danny Franklin while working as a dancer at Disney World (Danny played the Disney character Goofy in all the shows there). They had become close friends; then later they'd gotten sort of romantically involved. Danny was very shy—well, lately he'd begun to seem much braver—but still, Sam had ambivalent feelings about a romance with him. She'd always known that he was crazy for her, and that kind of scared her. So she'd told him she only wanted to be friends. Then, when he'd announced that he'd found another girlfriend, Sam had gotten totally jealous.

"I must be out of my mind," Sam said to the pitch black ceiling. "Why do I keep doing this?"

She turned over irritably and folded

her pillow again. "Here I am talking to myself, all alone, and Becky Jacobs spent tonight kissing Ian Templeton!"

Sam sighed and tried to get comfortable. She remembered a conversation she'd recently had with Emma and Carrie, in which she'd bemoaned the sorry state of her love life.

"I really think that for some reason you're afraid to be in love," Carrie had told her. "So every time you get close to a guy, you pull away."

Could that be true? Sam wondered to herself. *But I want to be in love! At least, I think I do!*

Sam snapped on the light switch, got out of bed, and walked over to the window. She stared wistfully out at the full moon.

"So, what's the deal Mr. Moon?" she whispered softly. "Am I afraid of love because I'm adopted? Or because I never met my birth father? Or is all that just a big, fat excuse?"

The man in the moon just kept the same maddening grin on his face.

"I guess you don't have any answers

for me, after all," Sam finally said. Then she went back to bed.

But sleep was a long time coming, because Sam couldn't stop trying to figure out what it was she really wanted from Danny, or Pres, or love.

TWO

"I guess we're all here," Billy Sampson said, looking around the somewhat ramshackle living room of the house on Dune Road, where all the guys in the band Flirting With Danger lived.

Billy had called an emergency band meeting for noontime, and Sam and Emma had both arranged to take a half-hour from their babysitting at the country club to come to the meeting. Carrie had to work, but Sam had called her earlier in the morning to see if she had any idea what the meeting was about—Carrie and Billy were a major league item—but Carrie had told her she didn't have a clue.

Yowza, my life changed when the Flirts picked me and Emma to sing backup for

21

them, Sam recalled as she looked around the room. *But these mysterious meetings always make me nervous. I'm always afraid they're going to fire me. Maybe it's because they almost did fire me once—of course it was my fault—but I guess I'm still freaked out by it.*

Sam smiled at Pres, who was sitting on the couch with Billy. He smiled back, then leaned over and said something to Billy. *Is it about me?* Sam wondered. *No, I'm just being paranoid.*

Pres glanced over at Sam again, and she peered at him to see if there was any of the warmth and even love that she used to see in his eyes when they'd been a couple. Her heart sank when all she saw was bland, professional friendliness. Emma's eye caught Sam's and Sam gave her a big everything-is-fine grin so no one would know how concerned she really was.

"So, what's up?" asked Jay Bailey, the laid back keyboard player for the group. He occupied one of the overstuffed chairs to Sam's left. Jay was quiet on the outside but something of a wild man on the inside, and Sam really liked him. She also thought he looked a lot like the rock legend James Taylor.

"Yeah, what's up?" Diana De Witt echoed. She was plopped on the floor near Pres and Billy. The third backup singer that the Flirts had chosen, Diana was one of the girls' archenemies on the island—Diana's best friend Lorell Courtland being the other. Diana was gorgeous, perfectly aerobicized, and totally hateful to Sam, Emma, and Carrie. She and Emma were old classmates from the Aubergame boarding school in Switzerland, and for some reason Diana lived to make Sam, Emma, and Carrie's lives miserable. Sam's eyes narrowed as Diana reached over and casually draped her arm around Pres's leg.

"We need to deal with some band business," Billy began.

"Wait a sec," Sam interrupted. "Where's Sly?" Sly Smith was the drummer for the Flirts', and he wasn't in the room.

"I thought Billy was running this meeting," Diana said sweetly, looking archly at Sam. She leaned her head against Pres's leg.

"He is, so why don't you shut up?" Sam spat at Diana.

Diana looked up at Pres. "What did you ever see in her?" she asked him with wonder.

"An IQ," Sam barked. "Unlike you I actually have one."

"Now that is so funny—" Diana began.

"CUT IT OUT!" Billy commanded. Both Sam and Diana fell silent. "We don't have a lot of time. This meeting is about Sly."

"Which explains why he's not here," Diana put in, looking coolly at Sam, "which you would know if you kept your mouth shut."

"Sly's sick," Pres said, ignoring Diana. "Really sick."

"Sick like he has the flu, or sick like he's in the hospital?" Emma queried with concern.

"Like the hospital," Billy confirmed. "He's got pneumonia. In fact, his parents just flew him home to Baltimore so he can see some specialist at Johns Hopkins."

"Why would he need a specialist for

pneumonia?" Emma asked in a soft voice. "Pneumonia isn't that serious."

"This pneumonia is," Billy replied, running his hand through his hair nervously. "Anyway, I've got an address for him, so we can all write, send flowers, that kind of stuff."

"God, this is awful," Sam said. "How soon will he be back with us?"

Pres and Billy exchanged looks. "We don't know," Pres finally said.

Diana cocked her head at Billy. "Are you telling us everything?"

"We're telling you all we definitely know at this point," Billy said. "We know that Sly is definitely not going to be with us for a while."

"Which is why we've got a new drummer," Jay announced.

"Wait a sec," Sam interrupted. "Is Sly gonna be okay?"

Billy looked a little grim. "I hope so," he said. "I really hope so. Meanwhile, we've got to go on."

"So we wanted to introduce you guys to our new drummer," Pres said.

"Nick!" Billy called loudly, "Come on in."

Sam saw an unbelievably handsome guy stride into the room from the back of the house, where he'd obviously been waiting.

"Flirts, I want you to meet Nick Trenton, who's going to be handling drums for us. Nick, this is the band."

Nick smiled confidently. He was about six feet, three inches tall, wearing jeans and a black T-shirt that read SURF COUNTRY on it. He had longish, straight brown hair and intense blue eyes. He also had a tattoo on each arm.

He is gorgeous, Sam thought. She shot a quick look at Diana. Diana was checking Nick out with great delight.

"Welcome," Diana purred, grinning at Nick. "We're really glad to have you."

Yeah, I bet she'd like to have him, Sam thought derisively.

Nick smiled back at Diana, but sat on the opposite side of the room, not far from where Sam and Emma were sitting.

Billy started to explain that they were lucky to have found Nick, that he had played drums with some of the best-known metal bands in the country, and that it was only by a stroke of good fortune that he was spending the summer in Kennebunkport down the coast and agreed to come help the band through this tough time. Through Billy's whole talk, Nick just sat there, exuding quite confidence.

Major-league cute, Sam thought, covertly checking Nick out.

"So, any questions?" Billy asked. "None? Good. We rehearse tomorrow, usual time. See you there."

The band members all stood up to leave. As they did, Nick turned to Sam. Sam's stomach turned to jelly.

"Hey," he said easily.

"Welcome aboard," Sam replied, her stomach now transformed from jelly to butterflies.

"Maybe we could get together sometime," Nick continued. "Get the lowdown on the island, et cetera et cetera blah blah blah."

Sam smiled. "Maybe," she said saucily, pleased that Diana was watching Nick talking with her. Then she saw Pres looking over at her too, on his way out of the room. *If I want to have a chance to get Pres back, I have to stop playing games,*

Sam told herself. She turned back to Nick. "And then again, maybe not."

"I heard the maybe," Nick grinned. "That's good enough for me. We'll talk about it tomorrow, if you call me. I'm at the Beachfront Motel. Meanwhile, I'm going to the beach. You work?"

Sure I work, Sam thought. *But I'm not going to tell this guy that I work as an au pair, a sort of glorified babysitter!*

"Sure," Sam responded easily. "Domestic assistant."

"Babysitter!" Diana yelled from across the room. Nick turned to her, ice in his eyes.

"Excuse me, but was I talking to you?" he asked coolly.

"No," Diana replied, clearly unphased, "but Sam's a known liar. I thought I'd save you the trouble of finding out."

"Did I ask you?" Nick questioned, his cold eyes still on Diana.

"Well, no," Diana said, beginning to squirm, "but—"

"Then kindly shut up," Nick said. "Didn't your mommy and daddy teach you any manners?"

"Hey, you can't talk to me like that!" Diana protested.

"I just did," Nick pointed out. He turned back to Sam. "Is she always like that?"

"Yup," Sam replied. "Only worse."

"Stuck-up rich bitch," Nick surmised.

"More or less," Sam agreed, grinning smugly at Diana, who flounced out of the house.

"Anyway, I'll be at the south end of the beach today," Nick continued. "We'll talk." He turned and headed back to the kitchen of the Flirts' house, where Billy, Pres, and Jay had gone when the meeting had ended.

Sam turned to Emma. "Oh my God," Sam said. "Did you just see that?"

"Sam . . ." Emma cautioned her.

"We are talking serious B-U-F-F! And he shut Diana up. You think he's human?" Sam asked, grinning widely.

"I think he's human and I think you should be careful," Emma replied. "You don't even know the guy. And I can see what's happening already."

"Please," Sam retorted. "I can take care of myself. For example, I am now

29

going to go back to work. And so are you."
Sam took Emma by the arm, and pulled
her gently toward the front door.

"Look, I just want to say one more
thing," Emma said when they got outside. "Just keep in mind that you and
Pres will never get back together if you
flirt with Nick."

"I wasn't flirting with him—he was
flirting with me!" Sam exclaimed.

"Sam, you know what I mean," Emma
replied, fishing her sunglasses out of her
purse.

"Well, maybe it would be good for Pres
to see me with someone else," Sam
pointed out.

"The only way it would be good is if you
want to break up with him forever,"
Emma stated, her arms folded.

"Well, maybe I do," Sam said. "Maybe I
want to be with Danny. Or maybe I don't
want to be with any one guy."

Emma shook her head ruefully. "In
other words, you don't know what you
want."

"Yeah, I guess," Sam admitted. "But is
that so bad? I'm only nineteen years old!

Why do I have to get so serious and everything?"

"You don't," Emma allowed. "I just—"

"Just quit worrying!" Sam interrupted. She gave Emma a hug. "I'm fine! I'm just having fun, and I'm not hurting anyone!"

"Okay," Emma replied, though she didn't sound as if she meant it.

"I'll call you later," Sam promised, as she headed for the Jacobses' car.

As Sam drove back to the country club, her mind kept returning to just one thing: how she could wangle some more time off that afternoon, so she could take a leisurely stroll—in her new black nearly-backless tanksuit—down to the south end of the main beach.

"Pneumonia?" Carrie repeated. "Sounds serious. Especially if he has to go into the hospital."

Carrie, Emma, and Sam had met up the night of the band meeting at their usual meeting place—in a booth under one of the video monitors at the Play Café on Main Street in downtown Sunset Island. The Play Café was a combination bar/restaurant/gameroom where almost all the young people on the island hung out—it was famous for its pool tournaments, and also because a lot of bands and musicians used it to try out new material in an intimate setting. Per usual, this evening, the place was packed.

"I had pneumonia once," Emma told them. "I just stayed in and they gave me antibiotics."

"Where were you?" Sam asked her.

"In the Alps," Emma explained.

"Of course," Sam replied. "You wouldn't get it in some boring place!"

"You have any idea what kind of pneumonia it is?" Carrie asked.

"I didn't even know there were different kinds," Sam replied, sipping her Coke. She looked around the cafe. "Where's Patsi?" she asked. "We ordered that pizza a long time ago!"

"Well, there are different kinds of pneumonia," Carrie replied. "I see Patsi over at that table near the jukebox," she added.

Sam waved at Patsi, their favorite waitress, who gave Sam an I-see-you-but-I'm-too-busy-to-get-over-there-right-now look.

"I'm gonna die of hunger," Sam grumbled.

"She'll get over here when she can," Emma said.

Sam turned back to her friends. "Listen, Car, you should see the replacement drummer they found. We are talking seriously fine. He makes every guy on this island look like dogmeat!"

"Make way, make way. Here's your pizza and don't say I never did anything for you," Patsi said, setting their pizza down on their table.

"Thanks, Patsi," Carrie told her. "You're a gem."

"I'm gonna quit this job. I swear to God," Patsi said, setting some paper plates and napkins on the table. "If I didn't spend so much money on clothes I'd be outta here." She sped away from their table.

"Yum!" Sam exclaimed, taking a large piece of pizza dripping with cheese.

"So this new guy is really gorgeous, huh?" Carrie asked Sam, helping herself to a slice.

"A major babe," Sam pronounced.

"I thought you said you were going to try to figure out what you want to do with Danny and Pres before you involved anyone else," Carrie reminded her. "At least that's what you told us a couple of days ago."

Sam looked at her archly. "Do you and Emma compare notes or something?"

"Well, you're the one who told us that," Emma reminded Sam.

"That's exactly what I am doing." Sam licked some tomato sauce off her little finger.

"Not if—"

"Please," Sam said. "For your information, I have been pondering the situation late into the night."

Emma chewed daintily on her pizza. "Well, that's a start, anyway."

"I'm confused," Carrie said, sipping her diet Coke. "Is it Pres you want or Danny?"

"Or Nick?" Emma added.

"Three guys for every girl?" Sam asked.

Carrie and Emma stared at her.

"Okay, okay," Sam said with a sigh. She put her slice of pizza down for a second. "I'm trying to figure things out. I really am. Now, am I mature, or what?"

"What," Carrie replied.

"Very funny," Sam said, reaching for her pizza again. "Hey, how's Adam?" she asked Emma, deftly changing the subject.

Adam was Sam's half brother. Sam, who was adopted, had recently gone to California with Emma and Carrie to visit her birth mother. There she'd met Adam, a twenty-one-year-old aspiring filmmaker. Emma and Adam were on the verge of a relationship after meeting again in New York City. But Emma was holding back, still getting over her relationship with Kurt Ackerman. Things with Kurt and Emma had almost gone the other way. The two of them had almost gotten married.

"He called me a couple of days ago from New York," Emma reported.

"And?" Sam prompted.

"He's wonderful," Emma reported with a smile. "He is being so understanding about my wanting to take everything slowly. I really appreciate the way he—"

"Hello, Sammi, darlin'!" cooed a singsong southern-accented voice from behind the girls. Sam groaned. It had to be

Lorell Courtland, the other half of the Courtland–De Witt duo. If sugary-voiced Lorell was around, Diana couldn't be far behind. And she wasn't.

"Why, it's the three musketeers," Lorell said, approaching the table. "How's the I-always-get-dumped trio doing?"

"It's so sad for you three," Diana added, coming up beside Lorell. "Kurt dumped Emma, Pres dumped Sam, and Billy is about to dump Carrie for someone I know and love—meaning me."

"Why don't the two of you go crawl back in your hole?" Sam asked brightly.

"Oh wow, Lorell," Diana said, "I think she was trying to insult us."

"I am positively cut to the quick," Lorell said gravely.

"I saw you making the moves on Nick today," Diana said to Sam, a nasty tone in her voice. "We all saw."

"He started talking to me," Sam reported.

"Funny, that's not how I remember it," Diana shot back. "Or Pres."

"You leave Pres out of this," Sam said angrily.

"Why Sammi," Lorell purred, "he's not your boyfriend anymore. Why should you care?"

Just then a new video came on the monitor, and someone cranked the volume all the way up. Diana tried to say something, but was drowned out by the raucous rock and roll. So she just shrugged, tapped Lorell on the shoulder, and the two of them gave exaggerated waves and blew kisses at the three friends, and walked away.

How to ruin a nice evening in three minutes, Sam thought, as Lorell and Diana strode to the bar. *They should take out a patent.*

Sam looked over at Carrie and at Emma. From the look in their eyes, she could tell they were thinking the same thing she was.

THREE

"Diana could get hit by a bus," Sam mused out loud. "Lorell could try to save her, and get run over by another bus."

This was about the hundredth fantasy death Sam had concocted for Diana and Lorell as she drove back to the Jacobses' house. By the time she pulled into their driveway, it was almost midnight and she was thoroughly depressed.

She sat in the car a moment, staring out at the night, deep in thought. *I don't have Danny, but I could have him as my boyfriend if I want him, but I'm not sure if I do. I don't have Pres, and I'm totally confused about that because when I see him in band meetings or band practice he makes me forget all about Danny. Why is that? And then there's this new guy Nick,*

39

who I tell myself not to think about, but it's like telling myself not to think about food. I'm still totally confused. I suppose that out of all of them, she thought, *I'm most serious about Danny. But how can I be sure? There's only one way to find out!*

Impetuously, she ran into the house and picked up the nearest phone, which was in the den. She dialed Danny's number in Florida. If he answered, it would be the first time she'd be speaking with him since she came back to the island from New York. Of course, she knew she'd be totally bummed if he didn't answer—that would probably mean he was out with Megan Carmony. The phone rang four times before someone noisily lifted it off the receiver.

"Hullo?" Danny said sleepily.

"Hi, Danny," Sam said, in as sultry and sexy a voice as she could muster. "It's not Megan Carmony."

"Sam," Danny murmured groggily. "I was fast asleep."

"Alone, I hope," Sam quipped.

"Yes, alone," Danny replied sleepily. "Just a sec—let me sit up. . . . There, much better. Hey, I'm glad that you called me."

"So . . . miss me?" Sam asked. Danny and she had gotten to spend a fair amount of time together when she was in New York with her friends. He'd told her he was dating some girl named Megan Carmony—someone he might even be getting serious about—but then he'd referred to Sam in public as his "girlfriend."

"Yeah, I miss you," Danny answered honestly.

"You seeing Megan?" Sam asked, unable to control herself.

"You don't want me to answer that question, do you?" Danny asked, sounding more awake.

Sam sighed. She remembered how shy Danny used to be. Clearly, he was becoming more self-assured. Sam sat down on the couch and twisted the phone cord around her finger. "Not really," she admitted.

"So, who are you seeing?" Danny asked Sam.

"Oh, no one in particular," Sam answered evasively.

"Just whatever comes along, huh?" Danny asked her caustically.

"That's not fair!" Sam exclaimed. "Would you feel better if I told you I was seeing one special guy?"

"No," Danny admitted.

"You know I really care about you," Sam told him in a low voice.

"Yeah," Danny said. "I know, Sam. But you're still confused, right?"

"Right," Sam admitted.

"So you called me at midnight to tell me you're still confused?" Danny asked her.

Sam bit her lower lip. "I think I liked you better when you were shy. You know that?"

"I'm still shy," Danny replied honestly. "But at least I'm really talking to you, which is good."

"Right, it's good," Sam echoed.

There was silence on the line.

"Look, Sam. It's okay if you're confused," Danny finally said. "Just don't take forever to figure out your problems. But I'll be your best friend until then. Scout's honor!"

"I do the best I can with my limited

resources," Sam joked, trying to lighten up.

Danny laughed.

That's one of the great things about him, Sam thought. *He always gets my jokes.*

"So . . . how's life?" Sam continued.

"Kind of boring, the usual Disney World stuff, you know," Danny replied honestly. "My grandparents were just here visiting. Hey, speaking of grandparents, have you heard from yours?"

"Not yet," Sam replied. "I hope soon. I mean, how could they resist me?"

A few weeks earlier, Sam had gotten up her courage and sent a letter to her biological grandparents—whom she had never met—in Israel. Her biological mother, Susan Briarly, had given Sam their address quite some time before, but Sam had never been willing to write to them.

What could I possibly say to them? she had thought. *That I am alive, and that I know their son Michael—my biological father—was held prisoner in Lebanon, or Syria, or whichever of those Arab countries it is—I can never remember.*

Then, Sam had changed her mind after talking to Danny about it in New York. Danny had said that he thought Joseph and Lillian Blady, Sam's grandparents, would be happy to know the truth—that the line of the family would be carried on, no matter what happened to Michael. Danny was Jewish, just like Sam's biological father and mother. He said he thought that Michael's parents would be very receptive and welcoming to Sam.

Sam was finally convinced. So she'd written to them, and, before she could change her mind, posted the letter. So far, there had been a couple of weeks of silence.

"Call me if you hear anything," Danny advised her.

"You got it, since you're responsible for this," Sam mock-accused him.

"I'll take the credit," Danny replied.

Danny and Sam talked a little while longer, then Danny pled exhaustion, because he'd run in a Disney character mini-marathon at Disney World that day, in costume. And it had been eighty-five degrees in the shade.

"Hey, I'm really glad you called," Danny said softly before he hung up.

Sam walked slowly upstairs and plopped herself down on her bed. She closed her eyes and sighed. *How come my life is so mixed up?* she wondered.

Her eyes popped open and she stared up at the ceiling. "I wish I was more like Carrie!" she said out loud. "She is so much more together than I am!"

Sam reached over and opened the drawer in her nightstand, and she pulled out a well-read piece of paper. For some reason, she had decided to make a copy of the letter before she had sent it off to Israel, and now, at twelve-thirty at night, she reread it for about the thirtieth time.

Dear Mr. and Mrs. Blady,

My name is Samantha Bridges. Actually, that's my adopted name. My adopted parents are Vernon and Carla Bridges, who live in Kansas. That's a state in the middle of the United States. Do you know it? I only found out recently that I am adopted. My actual mother, I have learned, is a Jewish woman in California named Susan Briarly. You know her, I think. I met Susan recently. She told me about Michael and her, and about you two. Well, I don't know any other way to say this than just to say it. I'm Susan and Michael's daughter.

I don't really know what I want you to say or expect you to do, except to know that from what I know about you I am proud to be your granddaughter. I really like Susan, and I am sure that I would have really liked Michael too if I'd ever had the chance to meet him. Susan told me I look just like him. She also told me what happened with him in Lebanon, so I know that I never will actually get to meet him, but I wanted you to know how I felt.

If you want to write me back, I would be happy to tell you more about myself. I have recently become pretty interested in my own history—I didn't even know that I was Jewish until this summer!—so anything you want to tell me, I will be glad to know.

I am enclosing a picture of myself, taken recently in New York City. I'm cuter than this photo, but I was squinting into the sun. Do you think I look like Michael? I really do hope you decide to write to me, but I guess I'll understand if you don't.

Sincerely,

Samantha (Sam) Bridges

Each time Sam reread the letter, she was amazed. *This is, like, the most honest, most straightforward thing I ever wrote or said in my life,* she realized. *Maybe I'm not quite as messed up as I think I am.*

She stuck the letter back into the drawer and began to get undressed. *I really, really, really hope they write back to me,* she thought as she dropped her clothes on the floor. *But somehow, I doubt they ever will.*

"Come on," Sam said to Carrie and Emma late the next afternoon, "It's just a walk down the beach a ways. You gotta come with me."

"No way," Carrie replied, her face deep in a novel called *War and Remembrance* by a writer named Herman Wouk, "this book is too good."

"Please, it's got a million pages. How can you stand it?" Sam snorted.

Carrie just shook her head and kept reading.

"Emma?" Sam wheedled. "I'll be your best friend!"

Emma shook her head. "I've got to go get Katie at the club in fifteen minutes." She cocked her head at Sam. "You're going to meet that guy Nick?"

"Not 'meet'" Sam explained innocently. "'Meet' would be a real overstatement. I might just happen to run into him."

Emma raised her eyebrows. "You might? What does that mean?"

Sam grinned. "Well, it might mean he doesn't actually know I'm coming, so it's not a meeting."

Sam had the rest of the afternoon free, because Dan Jacobs had decided to take his twin daughters on one of his periodic guilt-driven shopping sprees. Usually he just handed them his credit card, which of course they greatly preferred.

"Well," Sam said, standing up and brushing the sand off her legs, "I'm outta here."

"Did you wear that new bathing suit for Nick?" Emma asked Sam pointedly.

Sam looked down at herself in the bright red bikini covered with pink peace symbols that she'd found the day before on sale at the Cheap Boutique. She had decided it was even better than the black backless wonder. "This isn't new," Sam replied. "I bought it yesterday."

"Oh, well, silly me," Emma said.

"Be careful," Carrie warned her, not picking her head up from the book.

"Of what?" Sam asked. "This is a public beach."

"And you are Sam Bridges, and a guy is involved," Carrie replied.

"You guys underestimate me," Sam said, putting her sunglasses on. "However, if I'm not back in half an hour, send out a search party. On second thought, don't send a search party; just leave us alone. This guy is seriously cute."

"And you're already seriously confused about Danny and Pres," Carrie reminded her.

"You know what your problem is?" Sam asked Carrie. "You are too young to be so practical."

Sam walked along the water's edge. The beach crowd thinned out as she reached the south end, and she started scanning the few people on the beach to see if Nick Trenton was around.

There he was! At the far end of the beach, leaning up against a surfboard stuck in the sand, wearing a wetsuit, was Nick. He had a cigarette in his mouth, and as Sam approached him, he smiled at her confidently. She couldn't help but notice what great shape he was in, and how cute he looked with his hair ruffled by the wind. Sam noticed a tattoo that read "Born to Die Young" on his forearm. She couldn't decide if it was cool or gross.

"You came" were his first words.

"I'm walking on the beach," Sam replied coolly.

"All the way down here? I doubt it," Nick answered, taking a deep drag on his cigarette. "You want a smoke?"

"Hate the stuff," Sam replied, pushing her hair out of her eyes.

"Good girl," Nick muttered sarcastically. "You surf?"

"Are you kidding? I was born in Kansas."

"Korea," Nick replied, flicking the ash of the cigarette.

"You're kidding," Sam said. "You don't look—"

Nick laughed. "Military. Both parents. Don't know where they are now."

"You don't know where your parents are?" Sam queried, astonished.

"And they don't know where I am, either," Nick said. He took a last puff on his cigarette and threw it in the sand.

The two of them were silent for a moment.

"So, how come?" Sam finally asked, truly curious.

Nick shrugged, not looking at Sam, his gaze fixed on the swelling waves.

"Look," Nick said, "I was hoping we could go out some time. So when you're ready, call me. At the motel."

"But—"

"Time to surf," Nick said, jumping to his feet and grabbing his surfboard. "Call me when you're ready."

51

Nick put his board under his arm, strode down toward the ocean, climbed on the board, and began to work his arms out in a crawl stroke. Sam stood transfixed, watching his effort.

Then she wrenched herself away. *What are you doing?* she asked herself. *All you need is to get involved with still another guy. Again! Besides, he wasn't even nice to you just now!*

Still, she couldn't tear herself away. She turned to the water and saw Nick out by the breakers. He was the only surfer out there in the cold Maine ocean. She watched him as he paddled furiously, caught a big wave, and rode in toward shore. It was an awesome sight.

Who is this guy? Sam wondered. She thought she saw him wave at her briefly, but it might have been her imagination. She watched him for quite a while, more intrigued than she'd ever allow herself to admit to anyone. Not even herself.

FOUR

"Close, Sam," Darcy Laken said. "You almost landed it right on the skull."

"Not close enough," Sam groused. "Molly put one right on top!"

Molly Mason grinned. "Beginner's luck. Or maybe I'm just attracted to skeletons," she added.

Everyone who was hanging out in the backyard of Molly's parents' house—Darcy, Sam, Emma, Molly, and Molly's parents, Caroline and Gomez Mason—cracked up.

It was late afternoon of the next day. Darcy Laken, a good friend of Sam, Emma, and Carrie's, had invited all three of them to an impromptu cookout at the Mason's house. Unfortunately Carrie had to work, but Sam and Emma had both been able to take a couple of hours off.

Molly's parents wrote B-grade horror movies—in fact, one had recently been filmed right on Sunset Island—and everything they ever did had a horror motif. They dressed like characters in *The Addams Family* and lived in a spooky, haunted-looking house on the top of a high hill. At the moment everyone, except Mr. Mason, was playing a variation on horse shoes in the backyard—trying to land black bowler hats on a skull. Sam was pretty sure the skull was a replica from one of the Masons's movies, as opposed to the real thing, but she was afraid to ask.

She watched as Darcy bent over to share a joke with Molly. *I really like Darcy,* Sam thought. *She's such a cool, direct, together girl. And she's psychic, or at least slightly psychic, which kind of comes in handy sometimes. God, I wish I was! Then maybe I'd know which guy I'm supposed to end up with!*

Darcy lived with the Masons as a companion to sixteen-year-old Molly, who had been confined to a wheelchair since she was in a car wreck about a year and a half ago. Actually, Darcy and Molly were best friends, so it worked out really well most of the time.

"You going to take a turn, or don't you want to get your hands dirty?" Darcy teased Emma.

"Ha," Emma scoffed good-naturedly. "I'll beat the pants off of you!

"Bingo!" Emma cried. "Got one!"

Darcy peered down the lawn at the hatted skull. "And so you did. It looks charming on Chauncey."

"Chauncey?" Emma echoed.

"That skull," Molly pointed out from her wheelchair. "He used to be a character named Chauncey McGillicuddy in one of Mom and Dad's films—*Hatchet for Breakfast*, I think it was. Chauncey scared little children who didn't eat their cereal for breakfast, and then he ate them alive."

"Who wants to eat?" Mr. Mason called from the grill.

"Gee, I seem to have lost my appetite," Sam said feebly.

"No!" Molly cried, feigning shock. "You of the bottomless stomach? Grossed out by the plot of some little horror movie?"

"I do have a certain reputation to maintain," Sam agreed solemnly. The smell of the grilled burgers and barbecued chicken perked her back up. "I guess I could put away two or three burgers at that."

"Raw and bloody?" Molly asked, wiggling her eyebrows in a sinister fashion.

"Well done," Sam replied. "Let's go and . . ." Then she noticed that Darcy's face had a strange look on it.

"Uh-oh," Molly said.

"What is it?" Emma asked Darcy with trepidation.

They all knew that look. It meant that Darcy was having one of her weird ESP flashes—flashes that she couldn't control, that just came out of nowhere.

"It's . . . something," Darcy said, her pensive eyes filled with a searching look.

Molly sang out the theme music from the old TV show *The Twilight Zone* that they all watched on cable TV. Sam and Emma, and even Darcy had to smile.

"What is the Great Beyond telling you?" Sam asked.

"It's the oddest thing," Darcy replied. "What time is it?"

Sam glanced at her Mickey Mouse watch. "Almost one o'clock," she reported.

"I've got the weirdest feeling we should go watch the news," Darcy said. "And I'm not big on the news."

"What's up?" Caroline Mason asked, as she and her husband walked over to them.

"One of Darcy's 'moments,'" Molly explained to her mother.

"Ah," Caroline said knowingly. She absolutely believed in Darcy's powers.

"Please tell me someone murdered Diana De Witt," Sam pleaded.

"Sam's going to grow huge hooters?" Molly prompted teasingly.

"Oh, very amusing," Sam scoffed. "I know! Emma's family lost all its money in a big poker game?"

Darcy shrugged. "Beats me. But I'm going in. Wanna join me?"

The whole group of them made their way inside to the Mason family room. It was probably the only family room in the state of Maine painted jet black, with black marble floors, skull-printed wallpaper and black lights everywhere. Mr.

Mason flipped on the TV with the remote control, and turned to CNN. The news came on.

"So, what's the biggie?" Sam asked after they'd watched for a few minutes.

Indeed, the stories reported were of a recent change in the gross national product, the prime minister of France's upcoming visit to the United States, flooding problems in the Far West, and a possible prisoner exchange between Israel and Syria that the United States was helping to negotiate.

My grandparents live in Israel, Sam thought. *And my birth parents met there.* She sighed. Again, she wished she could have met Michael Blady, her birth father.

The news ended and Mr. Mason flicked the TV off. "So?" he asked turning to Darcy.

She shrugged. "Beats me," she said matter-of-factly.

"So, you're not getting any kind of special feeling about any of that?" Emma asked Darcy.

"I thought maybe . . ." Darcy began. Then she shrugged. "No. Nothing. Let's go eat!"

But as they all left the family room to go back outside, Sam could see Darcy shaking her head. There was something odd about that TV news broadcast. Sam was sure that was what Darcy was thinking. But neither one of them could figure out what it was.

"Back lotion alert," Sam said emphatically.

"I'll do it," Nick volunteered.

"My kind of service," Sam replied. "Prompt and cute."

It was late afternoon the next day, and Emma, Sam, Carrie, Billy, and Nick were hanging out together on the beach after a band meeting to discuss new sets for an upcoming local tour. It was hot out, and the five of them had gathered on the south end of the beach for some fun in the sun. Nick had brought his surfboard, but the waves weren't very good, so Carrie and Billy were using it as a headrest.

Nick reached over for the tube of sunscreen and started rubbing the lotion into Sam's back.

Ahhh, Sam thought, *this is the life. The Jacobs twins would call Nick an awe-*

some surfer dude, and they'd basically be right!

"Hey, ya'll," said a familiar voice with a Tennessee accent, approaching them on the beach.

Sam looked up. Pres. He looked down at her. Nick continued to spread lotion on her back. In fact, the lotion was basically all rubbed in, but he had continued to stroke her back sensuously. And she hadn't minded one bit. Now, when she tried to catch Pres's eye, he deliberately looked away.

Emma looked over at Sam inquiringly, but Sam just shrugged.

"Pull up a seat, pardner," Billy said to his bandmate.

"Don't mind if I do," Pres replied. He spotted a free section of blanket near Emma, pulled off his shirt and relaxed.

"I think the lotion's worked in now," Sam said to Nick.

"Sure thing," Nick replied. Slowly, he withdrew his hand, trailing his fingers across Sam's side. Sam looked over at Pres. He was already deep in a quiet conversation with Emma. Sam strained to hear what they were talking about, but the sound of the ocean drowned them out. Sam felt a quick, sharp spark of jealousy.

They look great together, they really do, she thought. *I bet they'd make a great couple. And now there's no Kurt—or me standing in their way. . . .*

Emma laughed and Pres joined in. Sam felt that stab again.

Just quit it, she told herself. *It's totally over with him. What are you getting yourself all worked up over?*

"I'm goin' in," Nick announced, pointing to the ocean and jumping to his feet. "Anyone wanna come?"

"Me!" Sam said, a little too enthusiastically.

"Anyone else?"

There was no response from the group. They were all either baking in the sun or talking.

"Then let's go, little drummer boy," Sam said to Nick.

She took his hand, and led him down toward the ocean. At the last minute, she turned her head quickly to see if Pres was watching her at all.

He wasn't. He was still talking to

Emma. The two of them started laughing again and Sam saw Pres's hand wrap around Emma's shoulders for a quick hug as Sam's feet hit the cold Atlantic ocean.

Sam parked the car in the Jacobses' driveway. It was about eight o'clock. She felt sunburned and irritable, angry with herself for getting so worked up over Emma's talking to Pres. As it turned out, Emma and Pres had been exchanging notes about a new book that Emma was reading and Pres had already read. In fact, they had tried to draw Sam into the conversation when she got out of the ocean, but Sam had basically ignored them, pretending to go to sleep on her towel.

Well, that's what they claimed, anyway, Sam thought. *They looked awfully cozy for a discussion about some boring book.*

Sam unlocked the front door—clearly no one was home. She made her way into the kitchen and got a Coke from the fridge.

I don't know whether I'm happy or sad that Pres isn't more upset about me hang-

ing out with Nick, Sam thought. *I'm sad, I guess. Or maybe I'm just crazy. Or both.*

She noticed a note on the kitchen table. It was from Mr. Jacobs and said that he had taken the twins to see a movie in Portland and wouldn't be back until late. It also said that there was a letter for Sam that had come that day, and he'd put it under her bedroom door.

Hmmmm. Who would be writing me? Sam wondered. *It's probably Susan Briarly, but it might be Danny. Or Mom. They're the only ones who send me stuff.*

Sam ran upstairs and spotted the letter. She stooped to pick it up. The material of the envelope felt unfamiliar. She looked at the stamps, which were also unfamiliar.

Oh my God. It's a letter from Israel. That means it's a letter from my grandparents. Oh my God.

Without moving, Sam tore the letter open. There were three sheets of paper inside. One of them was covered with strange-looking markings, which Sam figured was a foreign language— probably Hebrew. There were two pages written in English. Sam scanned the first, shorter sheet quickly.

Dear Samantha Bridges,

My name is Yael Havirim, and I am a student of law at the Hebrew University here in Jerusalem. My family is close friends with Joseph and Lillian Blady. Because the Bladys do not speak English, they have asked me to translate the enclosed letter for you. I do hope to meet you someday.

Faithfully yours,

Yael Havirim

Sam turned quickly to the other letter, her heart racing and pounding.

Dear Samantha,

We are sorry that we cannot write to you in English, but we speak only Norwegian, French, Yiddish, and Hebrew. As you know we came to

Israel directly from the concentration camps after being deported from Oslo, Norway.

If you speak any of these languages please tell us, because then we do not need the kind help of Yael. In any case she is a lovely and smart girl and we are sure that her translation will be faithful.

It was a joy to receive your letter. We are only sorry that Michael is not here to share our joy. You of course know about what happened to him in Lebanon. It is a tragedy and we miss him. He was our pride and joy. You are privileged to be of his stock.

Samantha, we were so sure that we were going to die without descendants. We lost so many members of our family in Hitler's gas chambers. To receive your letter, to learn of you . . . this is surely a gift from God. We do not judge. We Jews are a small people and each Jewish life is precious to us.

Please write to us again. No, come to Israel to meet us. We are old and frail and cannot travel, but it would mean so much to us to meet you, to touch you, to know that you live.

The photograph you sent us—you do look so much like your father, Michael. We have framed it and look at it every day.

Shalom and may God be with you always.

Your grandparents,

Joseph and Lillian Blady

Sam read the letter over and over again. But each time it was harder, because her hands were shaking more and more, and tears were filling her eyes. Finally, the tears spilled over onto the page she was reading, and she had to sit down. Then the tears came stronger than ever, and flowed onto the huge smile of joy forming on Sam's quivering lips.

FIVE

"Hullo?" Sam mumbled, reaching for the ringing telephone, the bright glint of sunlight bouncing around her room. It was the next morning, and Sam had fallen asleep the night before with visions of her new grandparents in her head.

"Sam? It's Emma."

"What time is it?" Sam mumbled.

"Almost nine."

"Well, the king of the hill said I could sleep in 'cuz he and the monsters are on a—get this—spiritual hike, so who invited you to be my alarm clock?" Sam said hoarsely.

"Sam, I want to talk to you," Emma said, a note of concern in her voice. "About yesterday."

"What about it?" Sam asked, still a little foggy from having just been awakened.

"About me and Pres," Emma continued. "I wanted to be sure that—"

"No biggie," Sam cut her off. "Forget it. You were just talking to him. About books, right?"

"Right," Emma replied, though Sam thought she detected a note of discomfort in Emma's voice.

"And he's not my boyfriend anymore," Sam added. "Not at the moment, anyway." Somehow, all of her problems and questions about guys seemed just so utterly unimportant at that moment, now that she had received this letter from her grandparents.

"But—"

"Please," Sam cut Emma off again. "You're allowed to talk to him. And he's allowed to talk to you."

"I just didn't want you to think that he and I—"

"I didn't," Sam assured Emma. *I'm a liar,* Sam thought to herself.

"Because the last thing I want," Emma continued to explain, "is Pres."

68

"Okay," Sam agreed, sitting up a little in bed.

"I mean, I only like him as a friend. Honestly."

"Hey, I got the message," Sam said.

"Well, okay," Emma replied, "I just wanted to be sure."

"No problem," Sam said. "I've got other stuff on my mind. Listen to this. The most amazing thing happened to me yesterday."

"What?" Emma asked. "Wait, are you absolutely sure you're okay about yesterday?"

Now Sam sat up completely. "Emma, now you *are* starting to get me worried. If it was really no big deal, you would not be going on about this. Am I right or am I right?"

"You're not right!" Emma insisted. "Even if I were really attracted to Pres, I would never let anything happen because I know it would upset you."

"Look, can we drop it?" Sam asked. "Listen to this. You remember I wrote to Michael Blady's parents in Israel a few weeks ago, right?"

"Right," Emma agreed.

"I got a letter back from them!" Sam cried with excitement.

"You're kidding," Emma exclaimed. "That's amazing."

"Nope," Sam answered, reaching for the letter. "Listen to this." And she read Emma both the short note from the translator and the entire letter that Joseph and Lillian Blady had sent her.

"It's wonderful!" Emma marveled. "I am so happy for you! So what are you going to do?"

Sam considered. Last night, when she'd read the letter, she'd been so overcome by emotion that she hadn't really thought about doing anything at all.

"Good question, no answer," Sam responded.

"Want to get together to talk about it?" Emma asked.

"Yeah, I guess so," Sam said. "But we'd better call Carrie, too. If I don't tell her, she'll kill me. Besides, she's the sanest person I know."

"How about the Play Café tonight?" Emma asked.

"No can do, babe," Sam sighed, wiggling her feet under the covers. "Becky's going over to Ian's later, and Claudia and Graham are taking Chloe to some relative's house. So Mr. Jacobs asked me to chaperone the lovebirds."

"You? A chaperone?" Emma said with a laugh.

"It is the strangest. I agree," Sam replied. "Maybe dear old Dad is afraid his darling daughter, Becky, will jump Ian's bones without adult supervision. Joy."

"And to think she used to call Ian a nerd," Emma recalled.

"Love is blind," Sam quipped.

"So how come Carrie couldn't just supervise Becky and Ian?" Emma wondered aloud.

"Because—now, don't choke too hard—Mr. Jacobs is under the impression that Becky respects me and will listen to what I tell her."

Emma laughed. "You're kidding."

"Hey, what am I going to do, disagree with the guy?" Sam asked. "I work for him!"

"Let's just meet up at Carrie's then," Emma suggested. "If it's okay with Claudia and Graham."

"They're not around, so Carrie's run-

71

ning the show." Sam said blithely. "Anyway, they should be more concerned about Becky being all over their kid."

"Sam—"

"Just kidding, just kidding. Sort of. Anyway, I'll be taking Becky over at six."

"I'll try to meet you there," Emma replied. "Bye!"

Sam hung up the phone. Then she reached for it again.

I've got to call Susan in California, she thought to herself. *She'll be so excited! I guess she'll be excited. Maybe it'll just upset her. But I've got to call.*

Sam looked in her address book for Susan's number and quickly dialed it. It rang five times before someone answered it.

"Hullo?" said a gruff male voice.

"Carson?" Sam asked, assuming that the guy answering the phone was Susan's husband. Carson was almost always unpleasant to Sam, and when Susan had invited Sam to her home, Carson basically just did a disappearing act.

"Yeah," the voice said. "Who the hell is this calling so early?"

"It's Sam Bridges," Sam replied, surprised at the venom in Carson's voice. "And it's not that early. It's after nine o'clock."

"It's barely past six o'clock!" Carson spat out. "Haven't you ever heard of time zones? I assume you want to talk to Susan."

"Yeah," Sam managed meekly. "I'm sorry I—"

"Hold on a sec," Carson interrupted tersely. Sam could hear Carson yelling for Susan to wake up and pick up the phone.

That's weird, Sam thought. *They're married and it's six in the morning out there. How come she's not in bed asleep right next to him? Uh-oh. Sleeping in different rooms. Bad sign.*

"Hello?" Susan's kind voice asked.

"Susan, it's Sam. I'm sorry if I woke you."

"Sam, what are you calling at this hour for?" Susan asked, concern rather than anger in her voice. "Are you okay?"

"I'm fine," Sam said, her heart starting to race.

How's Susan going to take this? she wondered. *Especially now that it looks like she and Carson aren't doing too well. How much does she wish Michael was still alive?*

"So why are you calling at six—"

"Susan," Sam began, her heart pounding, "the most amazing thing happened."

"What?"

"I . . . I got a letter from Michael's parents in Israel."

"That's some story," Carrie marveled, after Sam had read her the letter she'd gotten from the Bladys and told her about her phone call to Susan.

"Kind of puts everything in perspective," Sam commented, carefully putting the letter back into her purse.

"You must feel great," Carrie said.

"Sort of," Sam said, looking to change the subject. She didn't want to get too deep into this without Emma around. *I need advice from both of them,* Sam thought. "Hey, look at the two of them," Sam said, cocking her head toward Becky and Ian.

The couple sat together on the underwater steps of the gorgeous heated pool in the Templeton's backyard, their arms around each other, laughing and tickling each other, then kicking water at each other and screaming. Ian leaned over and kissed Becky, then he looked shyly over at Sam and Carrie to see if they were watching. He ducked his head for a second, but then grinned.

"They're in love," Carrie surmised with a smile. She leaned over the edge of her chaise lounge and took a sip of the iced tea she'd made.

"Diz gusting," Sam commented, reaching for the bowl of popcorn that sat between their chaise lounges.

"What's wrong with it?" Carrie said. "Don't tell me you never kissed a guy when you were fourteen."

"Never," Sam replied. "I didn't kiss *a* guy. I kissed *lots* of guys."

"Practice makes perfect!" Carrie surmised with a laugh.

"Anyway, it's still disgusting," Sam continued. "The two of them having so much fun while my love life is a mess!"

"Well, that's your choice," Carrie pointed out.

"Oh, thank you so much, Miss Maturity," Sam replied.

From the pool Becky giggled and leaned over to kiss Ian again.

"I think they're sweet," Carrie said. "I'm happy for Ian—he's had a crush on Becky forever. She's probably the first girl he's ever kissed."

"I doubt Becky would say the same thing about Ian," Sam replied archly.

"You are such a Scrooge!" Carrie giggled.

"Put me in *Sunset Beach Slaughter* and give me a kitchen knife," Sam joked, referring to the movie the Masons had made on the island. "Hey look, here comes Emma."

"Hi," Emma said to them, as she strolled through the back gate of the Templeton's house.

"Nice outfit," Sam commented. "Your basic Boston-baroness-goes-to-an-evening-get-together look."

Emma had on white linen trousers and a white linen vest, with a peach camisole peeking out from under the vest. A narrow white ribbon held back her hair, and she had pearl studs in her ears.

"Oh, this?" Emma said, looking down at herself. "Jeff and Jane are taking the family out to dinner in Portland. I'm going, too, and I won't have time to change. Which means I can't stay too long."

"And here I thought you wore that outfit for us," Sam said with a sigh. She and Carrie looked kind of grubby in comparison, both in cut-off jeans and T-shirts. Sam's T-shirt was cropped at mid-torso, while Carrie's baggy T-shirt bore the Yale logo.

"Ian, cut it out!" Becky squealed in mock-outrage. She splashed Ian and the two of them jumped into the pool.

"Ignore them. They're having too much fun," Sam advised Emma.

Emma sat down on the edge of Sam's chaise lounge. "I got the weirdest call from Darcy right before I left the house."

"What?" Carrie asked, taking a big sip of her tea.

"She told me that she had another flash about watching the news."

"Doing what?" Carrie asked, puzzled.

"Yeah, just like the last time," Sam scoffed. She turned to Carrie. "She had this weird flash that we should all go watch the news two days ago. It was your usual boring news, though. Maybe Darcy's blown a fuse or something."

Emma and Carrie laughed.

"Well, she told me that if I was coming over here, we all had to watch the news at six-thirty," Emma reported.

"But I have so much to talk to you guys about, and you have to leave soon, and it's already . . ." Sam checked her watch, "six twenty-five!"

"But look at the times that Darcy really has had a premonition about something," Emma reminded Sam.

"We can't just ignore it," Carrie agreed, sitting up.

"Okay, okay, I'll do it," Sam said, "but do you think it's safe to leave the junior lovers here alone?" She indicated Becky and Ian with her eyes, who at the moment were tickling each other in the pool.

Carrie grinned. "Ian's in a state of bliss. He won't move."

"It's not Ian I'm worried about," Sam said pointedly.

"They'll be fine," Carrie assured her, getting to her feet. "Becky can't actually attack him in the pool without both of them drowning. Let's go check out Darcy's ESP."

The three girls trouped into the Templeton's family room. Graham had recently purchased a large-screen projection TV, so the girls plopped down on one of the comfortable couches and Carrie set the TV to CNN. The news was just coming on. The first story was about the prime minister of France's visit to the White House.

"He's cute," Sam commented, as they watched the president giving the prime minister a tour of the Rose Garden. "Old, but cute."

"You think anything in pants is cute," Carrie teased her.

The next story was about the military prisoner exchange between Israel and Syria. CNN showed a videotaped report from the Golan Heights that separates Israel and Syria. The reporter explained that the United Nations had brokered this exchange of 376 prisoners—both Syrian military and Palestinians—whom Israel had captured in various engagements in southern Lebanon, for nine Israeli soldiers who were known to have been captured at the same time. Because the Lebanese government existed in name only, the negotiations were with Syria, who currently had more than forty thousand troops in Lebanon.

"Bor-ing!" Sam declared, ready to turn the TV off.

"You just got a letter from Israel," Carrie reminded her.

"That's interesting," Sam scoffed. "This is boring."

"Just another couple of minutes," Carrie said.

Michael Blady was a prisoner, too, Sam reminded herself. *Yeah, but everyone assumes he was killed years ago!* she answered herself. Sam sighed dramatically and began to flip through a copy of *Rock On* magazine, only half-listening to the news.

This is so unfair, Sam thought to herself. *I really need their advice, and the two of them have their eyes glued to the news because Darcy thinks maybe we're supposed to watch it. Gimme a major break!*

The report went on and on. The video showed school buses filled with Syrians and Palestinians being driven right up to the fortified border between Israel and Syria, and the prisoners, all dressed in identical Adidas warm-up suits and sneakers, piling out of the buses and running across the border.

Then, the video switched to the Israeli prisoners, walking exhaustedly from Syria back into Israel, where they were greeted with hugs, kisses, and cheers by their comrades.

"One odd twist on this exchange," the reporter said in his voice-over, "is that while the Israelis were only expecting nine prisoners to be returned, ten actually showed up. CNN has no information at this time as to the identity of the tenth prisoner."

Sam looked up for a moment. Just then, the camera zoomed in on the faces of the freed Israelis. It stopped and focused on one prisoner in particular.

What Sam saw made her heart stop. He was tall, lanky, and had a red beard, and piercingly intelligent blue eyes. He looked like he carried the weight of the world on his shoulders, but was also obviously so full of joy at his freedom that he couldn't speak.

"Oh my God," Sam breathed, her voice shaking.

"What is it?" Emma asked her. "Are you okay?"

Sam stared hard at the image of the TV. *I will never forget this moment for the rest of my life,* she realized.

Because the tall, lanky, red-haired prisoner looked exactly like an older, male version of Sam herself.

SIX

Sam refused to move.

She was actually glued to the television news—she refused to go back outside with Emma and Carrie when the initial report about the prisoner exchange was over, insisting instead that all three of them continue to watch the news. She had Carrie set up the Templeton's VCR so that she could tape the CNN report if it came back on. Emma called the Hewitts and told them to go to dinner without her.

Sam was in luck. At the top of the next half-hour, CNN repeated the report, and Sam got it on tape. She watched it over and over again. She froze the tape on the final image of the Israeli soldier with the red beard and the blue eyes.

"It might not be him," Emma said gently as Sam watched the replay of the video for the third time.

"It is him," Sam replied in a steely voice. "I don't know how, but I know it's him. My father. Michael Blady."

She saw Emma and Carrie exchange looks, and knew they were concerned for her.

What if it's really not him? a voice inside Sam wondered. *There's nothing that's been on that identifies him. And the story is that he was on a spy mission in Lebanon when he was reported missing. Everyone assumed he was dead! That was so long ago. Am I setting myself up just to be let down?*

Carrie and Emma sat back down with Sam when the commentator on the news said they had more information on the unknown Israeli soldier. Each of them took one of her hands.

"The unknown Israeli soldier released by Lebanon has been identified as Michael Blady of Jerusalem. . . ." the commentator announced.

Sam burst into tears.

"Oh, Sam," Emma cried, hugging her friend. "I'm so happy for you!"

Carrie squeezed Sam's hand hard.

"I knew it! I just knew it!" Sam managed to croak out between sobs. And she had received a letter from his parents—her grandparents—not a day before. Now what was she going to do?

"How do you feel?" Emma asked her.

"How would you feel if the father you never knew you had and then you thought was dead just appeared on your television set from five thousand miles away?" Sam asked, her voice more full of wonder than anything else.

"Probably confused," Carrie decided. She handed Sam a box of tissues from the coffee table.

"Probably hungry," Sam corrected, blowing her nose hard. "Is there any food around?"

Emma laughed. "Sam, you don't change."

"Not my stomach, anyway," Sam said, smiling through her tears.

Carrie went into the kitchen, and came back shortly with a big box of Oreo cookies.

"I checked on Ian and Becky," she reported, tossing the whole box of Oreos at Sam. "They're still splashing around in the pool."

"Do they still have their bathing suits on?" Sam asked, only half-joking.

"Apparently," Carrie replied.

"Then my job is still safe," Sam cracked. The girls all laughed.

"Glad to see you haven't lost your sense of humor," Emma noted, holding out her hand for an Oreo. Sam reached into the box, plucked out a cookie, separated the halves so the cream sides of the cookie were exposed, and then gave Emma two pieces of the cookie.

"You were gonna do that anyway," Sam quipped, when Emma looked at her quizzically. "Everyone does."

"My mother wouldn't," Emma said.

"Your mother does not eat Oreos at all," Carrie said, matter-of-factly. "If she won't wear clothes off the rack, I can't imagine her eating anything out of a box!"

"So how do you feel?" Emma asked Sam again, biting thoughtfully into one of her cookie halves.

Sam considered, swallowing an Oreo. "God, I don't know. Like . . . like I've been given a gift, but I'm scared to open it. How's that?"

"Poetic," Carrie commented. "Very poetic."

"Hey, someone's here to see you guys," Becky said as she and Ian appeared at the sliding glass doors to the family room.

"And we wanted to tell you not to bother us for awhile," Becky intoned meaningfully, clutching Ian's hand.

"Who's here?" Carrie asked.

"Me!" Darcy Laken shouted triumphantly, stepping out of the shadows of the backyard shrubbery. "I thought I'd find you here."

"How'd you know we'd be—"

Darcy laughed. "I'd like to say it was ESP, but actually I called the Hewitts and they told me Emma was here with you guys."

"Well," Carrie said, "come on in. Sam and Emma are both here."

"That's what I heard," Darcy said, walking into the house.

"So, be sure not to bother us," Becky insisted. "We'll be in Ian's room."

Sam's antennae went up immediately. "I don't think so," she told Becky.

"Jeez," Becky snorted, more to Ian than to Sam. "You'd think we were going to do something illegal! We just want some privacy."

Privacy for what? Sam thought. *Becky Jacobs, you'd better keep your clothes on, or your dad will kill you and me both!*

"We're gonna work on a new song for the Zits," Ian finally admitted.

"Sssssh," Becky cautioned, "don't tell her. She'll probably come try to steal it for the Flirts."

"Have fun, guys," Sam offered, rolling her eyes a bit at Becky's notion. "Just be sure you write the song with the door open."

"But Sam—" Becky began.

"Look, it's my job, okay?" Sam said. "Fight it out with dear old Dad."

"You are so out of it," Becky chided Sam. "I mean, aren't you seriously embarrassed to be a policeman for the Parental Unit?"

"Mortified," Sam said dryly. "And remember, we're gonna have to leave in about an hour. Be ready."

Becky rolled her eyes and turned away.

"Write a hit!" Sam advised. She turned back to her friends. "Somehow the problems of the teeny set don't seem important to me right now."

"You saw it, didn't you," Darcy said to Sam, her eyes shining. "I was right!"

"How did you know—" Sam asked.

"Well, you told me something about the whole thing with your adoption one day at the beach," Darcy said. "And I remembered some things you said about your birth father, and then I saw the guy. He looks just like you!"

"Yeah," Sam agreed, a grin spreading across her face.

"So, what are you going to do now?" Darcy asked her eagerly.

"Eat more cookies," Sam decided, reaching for the box of Oreos.

"She's in avoidance mode," Carrie explained.

"Puh-leeze," Sam quipped. "I'm doing the best I can."

"So?" Darcy asked. "How do you feel?" Sam felt Darcy's violet eyes train on her.

And she felt all her usual defenses start to slip away.

That girl is powerful! Sam thought. "I feel . . . lucky," Sam began. "I never thought he was actually alive. I never thought I'd actually get to meet him."

"What makes you think you're going to meet him?" Darcy asked, in her usual direct fashion. Darcy rarely pulled any punches. She said what was on her mind.

Sam froze inside. After receiving that letter from his parents, she had just assumed that once Michael Blady knew about her, he'd embrace her the same way that his parents had.

I just figured that he'd send me a plane ticket, and I could go to Israel to meet him in the fall, she thought. *Then I'd know my father and everything would be all right.*

"Are . . . are you telling me you have a feeling—" Sam stammered.

"I'm not telling you anything like that," Darcy replied directly. "Just a thought, that's all."

Sam bit her lower lip and thought for a moment. "I guess I never thought about that. I mean, that he might not even want to meet me . . ." Her voice trailed off.

"Who knows what's going to happen," Darcy said gently. "Michael has just spent God knows how many years in a prisoner of war camp. It's going to be hard for him to readjust to the life and the people he *did* know."

"A friend of my dad's was a P.O.W. in Vietnam," Carrie put in. "He adjusted fine."

"Do you even know how he was captured?" Darcy asked. "What do you really know about him? I'm not trying to be hard on you, Sam. These are just questions you should consider. . . ."

Sam rubbed her eyes wearily. *Actually, I don't know much at all. Not more than what Susan told me, not much about Israel . . . I never even read that book that Susan gave me!*

When Sam had first gone out to visit her birth mother, Susan Briarly, in California, Susan had given her a book written by Michael's sister, a woman named Beth Davidson, called *They Survived*. This book was the author's account of how her parents—Sam's grandparents—had survived the Holocaust and made it to Israel after the Second World War.

Sam started to feel tears welling up in her eyes. *This is all too much for me,* she thought. *I just want to have fun, and not deal with all this crap! But it feels now like this crap is going to deal with me whether I like it or not.*

"I want to go home now," Sam pronounced. She stood up to leave.

"Want me to go with you?" Carrie offered.

"No," Sam said quickly. "I need to be alone. And to make some phone calls."

"I hope I didn't upset you," Darcy said quickly.

"No problem," Sam said. "You were just pointing out all the possibilities."

"Sure you don't want one of us to come with you?" Emma asked solicitously.

"Sure," Sam replied, trying to muster a grin. "Call me tomorrow. No, actually, at the rate things are going, watch the news again tomorrow morning. *I'll* probably be on it!"

Sam looked at the clock. She couldn't believe that just fifteen hours or so before, she had dialed exactly the same number that she was dialing from her bed right now: Susan Briarly's number in California.

Actually, it took Sam some time after she came back from Carrie's to get the courage to call. She took a long hot shower, put on an old Kansas State University sweatshirt, and listened to her favorite Graham Perry love song on her head phones to calm her nerves a little bit. She heard Becky and Allie fighting down the hall, but she did her best to block it out, and dialed the phone number.

"Hullo?" a male voice answered.

"Carson?" Sam asked.

"Yeah," he said tersely. "Who's this?"

"Sam. Sam Bridges. In Maine," Sam answered nervously. She hated talking with Carson. It seemed as if their relationship had gone from bad to worse. "I was wondering if I could—"

Click.

I don't believe it. He hung up on me, Sam thought. *What a total jerk!*

Mad now, Sam furiously punched in

the number again. It rang four times before Carson picked it up.

"Hello," he snapped.

"It's Sam again. You hung up on me."

"I didn't hang up on you," Carson replied testily. "The baby did it. What do you want?"

"To talk to Susan," Sam replied coldly. If he was going to be nasty, Sam was going to be just as nasty.

"She's not here."

"When will she be back?" Sam asked.

"Don't know."

"Can I leave a message for her, at least?" Sam asked, with exasperation.

"Sure," Carson replied, "but she won't get it."

"You won't take a message for her?" Sam asked incredulously.

"What I meant was she's not coming home tonight," Carson explained, sounding weary.

"So where is she?"

"I don't know," Carson replied, nastiness creeping back into his voice. "Why don't you call El Al?"

"El Al?" Sam asked, puzzled. "Who's that?"

94

"The goddamn national airline of Israel, that's who it is!" Carson exploded.

In that instant, Sam knew exactly what had happened at the Briarly house in California. A wave of remorse shot through her. *Susan knows about Michael and she's gone to Israel. I'm the cause of all this,* she thought. *It's my fault.*

"Listen Carson," Sam said quickly, "I just want to know where she is. Then I'll hang up. I've got to talk to her."

There was silence. Then Carson told Sam to try Motel 6 in Hayward. Susan might be there.

"But I thought you said—" Sam began.

"It was a joke," Carson said without a hint of humor in his voice. "Yeah, a big joke." Then he hung up.

I can't believe this, Sam thought. *I really can't believe this. It should be a movie. But it's actually my life!*

She got directory assistance for Hayward, California, and got the number for the Motel 6. She dialed it. The clerk at the switchboard told her yes, there was a Susan Briarly staying there. She would transfer the call.

The phone rang in Susan's room, and Sam waited for Susan to pick it up.

"Hello?"

"Susan, it's Sam," Sam managed to say, clutching the phone hard.

"Sam!" Susan exclaimed. "He's alive! Your father is alive!"

"I know. I heard it on the news," Sam said, gulping hard. "I couldn't believe it! But . . . he's not my father. I mean, my father is Vernon Bridges. He lives in Junction, Kansas and he likes to grow roses. . . ." Tears were streaming down Sam's face.

"It's okay, Sam," Susan whispered gently into the phone. "Everything is going to be okay."

SEVEN

I must be losing my mind, slowly but surely, Sam thought to herself the next morning, as she strolled along the water's edge. The beach was bathed in a harsh early morning light. The sun had just risen and was not far above the horizon.

Maybe I'm still sane. But if I am still sane, what am I doing out on the beach at this hour?

She sighed and kept walking. And though the surf was rough and crashing, she could just hear the tolling of the church bells at Our Lady of the Sea over the sound of the waves.

Six o'clock in the morning, Sam thought. *I haven't been up at six o'clock in the morning in ages, much less walking by myself on the beach. I'm probably just crazed from lack of sleep.*

She'd tossed and turned all night long. Finally, at five A.M. she got out of bed, wrote a note to the Jacobs family telling them where she was, borrowed one of the bicycles from the garage, and rode down to the main beach.

Now at the shore, Sam inhaled deeply and threw a shell out into the ocean. *Kinda peaceful when it's empty like this,* she thought.

The beach, normally filled with vacationers with their radios blasting, blankets set up, beach volleyball games underway, and Frisbees flying, was practically deserted.

A guy was jogging down by the water's edge, his golden retriever dog running behind him. The guy waved as he passed. Sam waved back but kept walking. Farther down the beach she spotted a maintenance truck, it's workers emptying the refuse cans from the day before and collecting some stray bottles left over from a late night party. Sam could tell that she was looking at the aftermath of a frat party because a flag with three

Greek letters on it was still stuck in the ground, waving in the morning breeze.

Sam spotted a few fishermen surf-casting. She was surprised to see a father flying a kite with his young son—Sam wondered briefly why they were up so early, and where the wife and mother was.

Maybe there isn't a wife and mother, Sam thought. *Or maybe there's a divorce, and he's got the kid on visitation, so he's packing in every activity he can think of. God, I never thought about stuff like this before. . . .*

Sam, dressed in a pair of faded blue jeans and a nondescript red sweatshirt, continued walking along, lost in thought. She thought about that amazing moment the day before, watching television, watching the camera come in on the face of a man who looked just like she did. She remembered the feeling shc'd gotten in the pit of her stomach.

And she remembered the weird phone conversation she'd had with Susan. It kept replaying over and over in Sam's mind. Susan was so happy that Michael was alive, and she kept insisting to Sam that everything was going to be okay. But when Sam told her how awful Carson had been to her on the phone, Susan clammed up. Yes, Susan said, she and Carson had had some recent "marital difficulties," but she absolutely denied that her being away from home had anything to do with Michael Blady.

"It's something else," she'd said to Sam.

Sam didn't believe her, but didn't challenge her. Sam did ask Susan whether or not she thought she should try to contact Michael directly.

"It's up to you," Susan had advised her. "I'm not going to."

"You're not?" Sam had been totally surprised. "But I thought for sure—"

"No, no I can't," Susan had insisted firmly.

"Why?" Sam had blurted out.

"It's private," Susan had replied, a short tone in her voice. And then she quickly ended the conversation.

After that, there were a number of phone calls Sam thought about making. To Danny in Florida, because he was her closest confidante. To Pres, because Pres understood all this adoption stuff better than anyone else, since he was adopted, too. To her parents in Junction, Kansas, because she was sure that they would eventually see the newspaper story and then start to worry.

But Sam never made any of these calls. She just turned out the lights in her room and tried to will herself to sleep. But it didn't work. Which was how she found herself walking along the main beach at Sunset Island, before seven in the morning.

She had covered nearly a mile, walking south, and now the beach area was almost deserted. On the water, Sam spotted a lone surfer, with a yellow and orange surfboard, wearing a black wetsuit with orange and yellow stripes.

She had a shock of recognition. It was Nick Trenton. It had to be Nick. She recognized the wetsuit, which Nick wore because the ocean temperature was only sixty degrees or so. She stopped and watched as Nick expertly turned his surfboard around, paddled hard to catch a wave, got right up on his board, and neatly rode one of waves in toward shore, executing a series of neat cuts and turns that showed he really knew his business.

Nick rode the wave nearly all the way in. At the end of his ride, he spotted Sam on the beach. Still on his board, he gave her a quick wave, and she could see a smile coming over his face. He dropped down to his board, gave a bunch of quick arm-over-arm crawl strokes, jumped off the board into water that came up to his thighs, grabbed his board, and walked slowly out of the ocean toward Sam.

"Hi!" he greeted her warmly. "Fancy meeting you here."

Sam smiled back. Nick's grin was infectious. "Oh, I'm always out here just about now," she replied breezily.

"Nope," Nick said, still grinning. "*I'm* always out here now. You never are or I would have seen you."

"Is that so," Sam remarked.

He gave her a cool look, but didn't reply. Then he looked back out at the ocean.

Sam stood there, waiting. *Why am I standing here flirting with him?* she asked herself. *I don't have to do this. I've got other things on my mind than this guy! I should just leave. . . .*

"Decent waves today," Nick finally said. "Want to try?"

Sam shook her head no.

"I could teach you sometime, maybe," Nick said. "Do me a favor, unhook me." He pointed down to his ankle, where a long rubberized tether that kept the surfboard from flying away from him if he lost balance in a wave, was attached by a Velcro band just above his ankle. "I'm too tired to move. I started at five."

Sam reached over and undid the tether.

"Thanks," Nick said. "Want some coffee? Let me invite you to Nick's diner." He pointed up the beach a little way, where Sam could see a blanket, a cooler, and a thermos sitting on the sand.

"No, thanks, I'm gonna keep on walking," Sam said.

Nick touched her arm. "You sure? Wouldn't some hot coffee be good?"

She hadn't had any coffee to start the day, and she was not used to being up at this hour. Her eyes felt scratchy from lack of sleep. "I guess coffee would be good," she finally said.

"Follow me," Nick pronounced. "This place has the best prices in town."

Sam followed Nick up the beach to his blanket. He told her to help herself to coffee in the thermos, which she did—it was steaming hot and black—while he peeled off the top of his wetsuit and dried himself with a towel. Sam checked out his broad chest.

This guy is a major babe, she thought to herself. *God, I am hopeless. I will be thinking about guys on my deathbed.*

"Sure I can't persuade you to try surfing sometime?" Nick asked, as he sat down next to Sam, reached into the cooler, and took out a box of donuts for the two of them to share.

"I've tried windsurfing," Sam replied. "I'll stick to that."

"No danger," Nick answered.

"That's the whole point," Sam grinned.

"I like to live dangerously," Nick announced. "So . . . what brings you out to the beach at this hour? No, I know. You came out to meet me."

Sam smiled. "Not a chance."

"Huh, and here I thought you were looking me over pretty good," Nick said, taking a sip of his coffee.

"You thought wrong," Sam said, taking a bite of a donut.

"So what then?"

"Oh, just, you know, things," Sam said evasively, running a finger through the sand next to the blanket.

"Hey, you can tell me," Nick said. "Sometimes it's easier to talk to someone you hardly know."

And then Sam astonished herself.

Sam remembered something that Carrie had once said to her: that it was amazing how people will sometimes just spill their guts, and tell their entire life stories, with the most intimate details, to people that they barely know.

Sam knew this was true. She had once taken a bus ride from Junction to Topeka and a matronly woman sitting next to her had regaled her with stories about her eldest son who was doing time in prison for murder, and how she herself was on her way to Topeka to be operated on for breast cancer.

Sam had vowed at the time that she

would never embarrass herself by being so forthcoming.

But now she hesitantly began talking. And once she started talking, she couldn't stop. And by the time she was done, Nick Trenton knew almost everything there was to know about Sam Bridges's family life; her parents in Kansas, her finding out about her adoption, and the recent revelation that Sam's birth father was alive in Israel.

"You know what I think?" Nick said, chewing thoughtfully on a donut.

"What?" Sam asked, a little ashamed at herself for having spoken so long to a guy she liked and was clearly attracted to, but who she didn't know very well at all.

"I think you need a nap," Nick said, matter-of-factly. "Right here, on the beach, in the sunshine. Chill out."

"That's your advice?" Sam asked. "Chill out?"

Nick nodded. "You are stressed to the max."

"I can't," Sam said, "I gotta get home. The girls—"

"The girls," Nick repeated derisively.

"Take it from me. Sometimes you need to look out for number one. Now, what time do you start?"

"Nine o'clock," Sam answered.

"No problem," Nick said, taking the waterproof watch he was wearing off his wrist, and setting the alarm part on it for eight. "I've set the alarm for eight."

"But—"

"No *but*'s," Nick replied. "This is Nick Trenton talking. I'm going back out there for a while. You sleep." Nick pointed to the blanket.

I really am exhausted, Sam thought. *That coffee isn't keeping me awake at all.* She nodded. And the next thing she heard was the *beep-beep* of Nick's watch alarm going off. She opened her eyes. Nick was asleep next to her on the blanket. And while they were napping, somehow his hand and her hand had gotten intertwined.

"Good morning," Nick grinned sleepily.

"Good morning," Sam replied, gracefully withdrawing her hand from under Nick's.

"What I want to know," Nick said, still grinning, "is whether our hands are trying to tell us something." Then he leaned over and gave Sam a soft, sensuous kiss. Without stopping to think, Sam found herself kissing him back.

Nick pulled away for a second and regarded Sam. Then he took her in his arms and kissed her until Sam lost track of everything.

"Hi, Sam," Becky Jacobs said cheerfully from the breakfast table, where she sat with Allie and their father, when Sam walked into the kitchen at eight-thirty, "Have you lost your mind?"

"That means she has a mind to lose," Allie quipped. "Not!"

"I know you went to the beach, but isn't it kinda hard to get a tan at this hour?" Becky asked.

"Maybe she was meeting someone," Allie suggested, pouring herself a glass of orange juice as she talked. "Someone really buff, a major babe-alicious hunk—"

"Pres already dropped her," Becky reminded her sister.

"Oh yeah, that's right," Allie said,

spreading some jam on her toast. "Never mind."

"Hi, Sam!" Dan said cheerfully, as always, oblivious to how rude his daughters could be. "Out getting some fresh air, huh?"

"Uh, yeah," Sam answered, very surprised that the Jacobs household was up and about so early. Normally, they didn't get up until after nine o'clock.

"We found your note," Dan reported.

"Duh," Allie cracked.

"Double duh," Becky added.

"What're you guys up so early for?" Sam asked, sitting down at the table.

"Dad's taking us on another spiritual nature walk," Becky said, making a face, and using the same tone of voice that she might have used to say "Dad's taking us to visit a firing squad, and we're the targets."

"It'll be fun!" Dan said gaily. "Didn't we have fun the other day, girls?"

"Oh, heaps," Allie replied, pouring herself more juice.

"We don't have a choice," Becky added morosely. "We have to go. It's assigned from school. Ugh."

Sam raised her eyebrows quizzically. "What do—"

Dan cut in. "The twins' school has given them homework assignments for the summer. One of them is a nature walk. What a great idea!" he exclaimed.

"I'm gonna hurl," Becky said sourly.

"It's bad enough you have to deal with school from September until June— What did they have to go and ruin my summer for?" Allie added.

"But I thought you *liked* nature," Sam said to Allie, remembering a camping trip they'd taken with Emma and the Hewitts earlier that summer. Allie had had the best time of anyone.

"Not when I have to do it for school," Allie answered.

Just then the phone rang. "Would you get that?" Dan asked Allie.

"No," Allie replied.

They are so unbelievably obnoxious sometimes, Sam thought.

"It's a stage," Dan said as if reading Sam's mind. "You probably went through it."

I don't think so, Sam thought.

Dan rose to get the phone.

"Hello?" Dan said, picking up the kitchen phone. "Yes . . . yes . . . Yes, she's here . . . You're calling from *where?* Hold on a sec." The kitchen turned quiet.

Dan held out the phone to Sam. "The call's for you," he said. "The guy has an accent, and he says he's calling from Israel."

EIGHT

Sam looked at Dan in shock. She was speechless.

"I'll . . . I'll take it upstairs," she finally managed.

"Is everything okay?" Dan asked her. "You're looking kind of white."

"Oh, I'm fine," Sam said in a faint voice that sounded anything but.

"Are you sure?" Allie asked, concern etched across her face.

"Sure," Sam replied, only barely registering that Allie was showing actual concern for her. "Excuse me." She ran upstairs and into her room, and sat down on her bed. She took as deep a breath as she could muster and picked up the phone.

"You can hang up now!" she called

downstairs, and heard the click in the receiver as she put her ear to the phone.

"Hello?" she said, in a quavery voice. *Oh God,* she thought to herself, *it's either him or his parents. It's one or the other, and I don't know whether to be happy or totally scared to death.*

"Samantha Bridges?" the strong voice with a foreign accent asked.

"Yes," Sam replied, her voice sounding tiny to her own ears.

"Ah," the voice said. "It is you. I am so glad. My name is Michael Blady. My parents told me you wrote to them. I think you know who I am."

Oh my God. It's him. It's him himself. I can't believe it. What am I supposed to say? What am I supposed to do? Sam thought, though her mouth was unable to form words.

"Yes," Sam managed. "I know who you are."

"You do not know the joy it is for me to speak to you," Michael continued. "I got your number from the return address on the letter you sent to my parents. I called your directory assistance," Michael said, his voice somewhat hesitant, sensing Sam's discomfort.

"I wrote to them," Sam said. *Gee, that's bright. He already knows that,* she thought. *He just said so!*

"It was courageous of you to do that," Michael replied. "You must be a courageous girl."

"I don't think so," Sam answered honestly.

"But you are," Michael responded. "Courage is important. You heard about what has happened to me?"

"It was on the news here," Sam said. "I watched it with my best friends."

"Your newspapers are calling me all the time," Michael replied. "And the news. And CNN."

"Oh," Sam answered, not sure how that was important to her.

"And the military wants to put me into isolation, for debriefing," Michael continued.

"What's that?" Sam asked, totally baffled.

"They want to ask me about my captors, whether I was tortured, the whole story," he said.

"Were you?"

"That is not to talk about now," Michael replied, his voice on the transatlantic phone link as clear as if he were in the room with Sam.

God. He was tortured. My birth father was tortured while he was a prisoner, Sam thought. *That is so horrible. And I have no idea what to say to him.*

"Your parents are very nice," Sam offered. "I mean, they seem nice. As nice as people can seem when you don't speak the same language. I mean, write in the same language." Sam winced. *God, I sound like an imbecile.*

"They are wonderful," Michael said.

"They must be very happy you're alive," Sam said. *Well, of course they're happy, that was a really dumb thing for me to say—*

"They think—how do you say it in America—it is awesome," Michael replied.

Sam laughed. feeling a little bit more comfortable for the first time. She was surprised that Michael would be using current American slang. "How do you know that expression?"

"My captors let us watch TV sometimes," Michael explained. "I have a good memory."

There was silence on the phone. Sam searched desperately for something to say. *I want to know a million things, and yet I can't even find the right words to say one stupid sentence!* she railed at herself. "Well, I guess this is a really great reunion with your parents," she finally said.

"I am so happy to see them," Michael said, "but they have changed. I remember them so much younger."

"I'd like to come to Israel sometime," Sam blurted out, "to meet them and to meet you." Then she remembered what Darcy had told her, that maybe Michael wouldn't even want to meet her. "Well, I mean, you wouldn't have to meet me if you didn't want to—"

"But of course I want to," Michael said softly. "That is why I called."

Sam sat down on her bed hard. "It is?"

"Yes," Michael replied. "I would like to come to America to meet you."

Sam gulped hard. "You would?"

"I know this is very sudden," Michael added. "Perhaps you don't want—"

"No, no," Sam said quickly. "I want to meet you. So much. I'll be on Sunset Island until the end of the summer, and then I'll probably go back to Kansas, unless I can find a job dancing. But you can come to wherever I am in the fall—"

"Tomorrow," Michael said.

"Tomorrow?" Sam echoed, barely comprehending.

"Yes," Michael repeated. "I would like to come tomorrow. If that is okay with you, of course."

"Tomorrow, as in the day after today?" Sam squeaked.

"I have already booked a flight from Jerusalem to Boston," Michael said quickly. "The government will allow me to visit for four days, then it is back for more debriefing. You have no idea how hard it was to convince them to permit this."

"Tomorrow," Sam repeated, realizing she was beginning to sound like a scratched CD.

"I know this is very sudden," Michael said, his voice full of emotion, "but it means so much to me to know that you exist. That Susan and I . . . well, to see you with my own eyes is very important to me."

"It is?" Sam asked.

"Very important," Michael maintained. "I insisted that they let me come to America. Then they can debrief me forever more. That is what I told them."

"How long a flight is it?" Sam asked.

"Long," Michael answered. "Eleven hours."

"Wow," Sam breathed. She had no idea that the Middle East was so far away.

"But it will be worth it," Michael said emphatically. "I know it will be. But I will not come unless—"

"I want you to come," Sam insisted. "I . . . I want to know you, and I never thought I would get the chance. But . . ." Sam bit her lower lip with anxiety. "I . . . I have a father. He loves me. He raised me. He lives in Kansas. . . ."

"I understand this, Samantha," Michael said solemnly. "I respect this."

"Okay then," Sam said, taking a deep breath.

"Are you sure?" Michael answered.

"You don't know me very well yet," Sam replied with bravura. "Nothing ventured, nothing gained. If it's an adventure, count me in. And this is an adventure."

"I am an adventurer, too," Michael replied. "But this is not an adventure. This, Samantha, is a miracle."

"He's coming when?!" Carrie asked, as Sam, she, and Emma were hanging out by the pool at the Sunset Country Club. It was later that day and Becky and Allie Jacobs were taking a dance class inside the main building, while Ian Templeton and Wills and Ethan Hewitt were engaged in something called the "Kwatic Kapers," an annual event at the club which consisted of various wacky water events. At the moment, all the kids were engaged in pushing balloons across the surface of the water with their noses in the shallow end of the pool.

"Tomorrow," Sam answered, in a tone that she would use to say that the carpet cleaners are coming tomorrow, pulling the straps down on her black bikini so that her shoulders would tan evenly.

"Tomorrow!" Emma exclaimed. "This is unbelievable! How do you prepare for something like this?"

"Prepare?" Sam asked. "What's that mean? I'm totally prepared right now. 'Michael, meet my two best friends in the world, Emma Cresswell and Carrie Alden. To know them is to love them.'"

Carrie and Emma laughed. "I guess you're right," Emma said. "There's probably not a lot you need to do."

"Just screw my courage up," Sam said. "That's all."

A big cheer went up from the pool. Ian Templeton had won the balloon push event. Now the kids were being herded into one corner of the pool—it looked like some sort of underwater running race was being organized.

"How long will he be here?" Carrie asked.

"Just a few days," Sam replied, spreading some lotion on her shoulders.

"Just long enough to get to know you a bit," Emma considered.

"Just long enough to meet Diana De Witt," Sam cracked. "Then he'll be sure to leave."

"So, how do you feel about this?" Carrie asked Sam, as she rolled over on her chaise lounge.

"Peachy," Sam replied. "Totally peachy."

"Sam . . ."

"I'm fine, honest!" Sam insisted. Her two friends stared at her. "Okay, I'm scared to death. Are you two happy?"

"Talking about how you really feel is not illegal," Carrie pointed out.

"No, it's just usually boring," Sam replied, reaching for a bag of mixed nuts she'd bought. "I mean, these people who go on and on about how they feel just make me want to hurl—"

"You are changing the subject," Emma said. "How do you feel?"

Sam thought a moment. "My stomach is doing flip-flops. I was on the beach at six this morning. I didn't eat breakfast."

"No" Carrie uttered. "You missed a meal?!"

"Well, I'm glad to see you're human," Emma remarked.

"Barely," Sam cracked, making a joke at her own expense.

There was another commotion from the pool. The water running race had just finished, and Wills Hewitt was shouting, claiming that he'd been cheated, and that he'd actually won the race. But the counselor in charge said no, that another kid had won. Tears were starting to course down young Wills's face.

"Your kid looks bummed," Sam said to Emma.

"To him," Carrie said, "losing that race is as important as . . . as your birth father coming here is to you."

"You think so?" Sam asked, popping another nut into her mouth. "I always think that stuff just slides off kids. I mean, they seem upset at the time, but then five minutes later, they're fine."

"Is that how you were at Wills's age?" Emma asked Sam.

"I was never Wills's age," Sam replied. "I was born a woman of the world." She poured the last of the nuts into her mouth and crumpled up the package. "God, I can't believe this is really happening. My birth father. He's Jewish. No, he's Israeli. And he's Jewish. And he's famous. And he's coming here to see me."

"So when's he getting here?" Carrie asked, turning over to sun her back.

"Late afternoon tomorrow," Sam said.

"Do we get to meet him?" Emma asked, excited.

"How about at night, at the Play Café?" Sam asked. "It'll be much easier if I can spend time with you guys while he's here. I mean, I don't even know him! English isn't even his first language!"

"I'm sure you'll be fine," Carrie said. "Anyhow, we'd love to meet him."

"Actually, on second thought," Sam mused, "let's skip it."

"Why?" Carrie demanded.

"Because I'm embarrassed about you guys," Sam said, deadpan. "You have no social skills whatsoever."

"Sam!"

"Okay," Sam said, laying back down on her chaise lounge, "you talked me into it." She looked over at Carrie and Emma. "Thanks, you guys. I mean it."

"Hey, to know us is to love us!" Emma quipped.

Sam laughed. "God, that sounds so funny coming from your pristine lips."

She sat back up. "Hey, speaking of lips, I didn't tell you guys about Nick!"

Carrie laughed. "I'm sure that follows—lips, Nick."

"Well, his are so great-looking," Sam shrugged. "Anyway, listen to this." Sam then explained how she had taken her early morning walk and met up with Nick. She told them about their encounter, including the part about how she had awakened on the beach with Nick's hand entwined with hers.

"He's a babe to the max," she concluded. "It's just what I need. I've got all this serious stuff in my life right now. I just want to have fun with a guy."

"Billy's told me some things about him," Carrie replied, her voice cautious. She scratched at a mosquito bite on her leg.

"What kind of things?" Sam asked.

"Not so good," Carrie admitted.

"For example?" Sam demanded, sounding dubious.

"He was arrested for busting up a hotel room with a band out on tour," Carrie explained.

"Big bad deal," Sam answered airily. "That's just rock and roll."

"And he was kicked out of another band," Carrie added.

"What for?" Sam queried.

"Billy doesn't know," Carrie admitted. "No one will talk about it. Including Nick."

"So what," Sam scoffed. "I got kicked out of Disney World."

"So?" Emma asked, joining the conversation. "At least you'll talk about it."

"What have you two got against Nick?" Sam asked. "It's not like I'm marrying him. Can I help it if the guy is awesome looking?"

"We don't have anything against him," Carrie answered. "At least I don't."

"So, then—"

"We know you, Sam," Emma interrupted her. "We don't want you to get hurt."

"Again," Carrie added.

"Listen, fellow foxes," Sam said, "Sam Bridges has a father who was a P.O.W. in Syria. I come from tough genes. I ain't getting hurt."

"Just watch yourself, okay?" Carrie

asked. "I don't have a great feeling about this guy. Neither does Billy."

Sam sat up and got a ponytail holder out of her bag and stuck her hair up on her head. "Then why did he hire him?"

Carrie shrugged. "They needed a good drummer, I guess."

"Look, if Billy really thought the guy was so bad, he wouldn't have hired him to replace Sly, right?"

"I guess," Carrie said, but she didn't sound convinced.

"Oh, I forget to tell you," Emma said, sitting up. "I got a card for Sly, which you two need to sign." She rummaged in her bag for the card.

"Have you heard how he is?" Carrie asked Emma.

"No, just that he's still in the hospital. Here it is." She handed the card to Sam, who quickly wrote a short note and signed her name. Sam passed the card to Carrie.

"Maybe we could call him or something," Carrie suggested as she signed the card. "I'll ask Billy about it."

"Hi, Sam!" a pair of voices chimed out from the far end of the pool. It was Allie and Becky, both wearing tiny cut-offs and bra tops. "We need you to drive us over to Ian's house," Becky added.

"Since when?" Sam asked.

"Since we just asked you," Allie said, as if she were talking to a moron.

"I meant since when did your dad say you could go to Ian's," Sam explained evenly.

"We just called him. He said it was cool with him if it was cool with Ian's parents. And Ian's parents aren't home, so that makes it all okay."

Sam laughed. "Gee, I don't follow that logic."

"That's because you are getting seriously out of touch," Becky told Sam, pushing her hair out of her face. "Let me explain slowly. Allie and I are going to Ian's. Allie is going to be with Kevin— this cute guy we just met—and I'm going to be with Ian. Got it?"

"Don't I have something to say about this?" Carrie asked mildly.

"I suppose," Becky sighed, her hand on her hip.

Carrie turned to Sam. "Want to come over with the twins?"

"She works for us, she has to," Allie put in.

"If you two don't stop being so obnoxious, I'm not going to do anything for you," Sam told the twins, "and that's a promise."

"Hey, who was it who called you from Israel this morning?" Allie asked Sam, completely changing the subject.

Sam hesitated a moment. The twins knew she'd found out she was adopted. In one of their rare warm and serious conversations she'd even told them that her birth father was Israeli, and probably dead.

"My birth father," she finally admitted.

Becky's and Allie's eyes got huge.

"He's alive?" Becky asked her.

"Yeah," Sam said.

"Oh, my God, that is so awesome!" Allie screamed, and she threw her arms around Sam. Becky ran over to her and joined in the hug. Sam was just about as shocked as she'd ever been in her life.

"Honestly, that is mondo-cool," Becky cried, her eyes shining. "So, like, are you going to Israel to meet him?"

"No, he's coming here," Sam told her.

"Wow, this is so great," Allie marveled.

Just then Ian and a cute blond-haired guy that Sam assumed was Kevin ambled over to the twins. Ian put his arm around Becky, and Kevin put his arm around Allie.

"You guys ready?" Ian asked the twins.

"Sure," Becky told him, snuggling against him. She turned to Sam. "We'll meet you by the car." The twins took off with the guys.

Sam turned to her friends. "Wait a second. Did that little conversation just take place? Were the twins really nice to me just now?"

"They were," Carrie confirmed.

"It's like *Invasion of the Body Snatchers* with them," Sam marveled. "One minute they're obnoxious, the next minute they're sweet."

"Maybe it's because their own mother kind of deserted them," Emma reminded Sam. "Parents are a big thing to them."

"Yeah, I bet you're right," Sam agreed. She stood up and stretched. "You ready to boogie on outta here?" she asked Carrie.

"Yeah," Carrie replied, gathering up

her stuff, "I just have to get Chloe from the kiddie pool."

Sam hoisted her pool bag on her shoulder. "Listen, I just want to thank you guys for . . . you know."

"No, we don't," Emma said. "What?"

Sam sighed impatiently. "For . . . listening to all this stuff about my birth father."

"Sam, we had to pry it out of you," Carrie reminded Sam.

"Yeah, that's true," Sam admitted. She thought for a second. "Well, thanks for caring enough to pry it out of me. How's that?"

Carrie grinned at Sam and reached up to loop her arm around Sam's shoulder. "That, Sam Bridges, is great!"

NINE

Where is he? Sam thought nervously to herself, as she sat out on the back deck of the Sunset Inn, uncharacteristically alone. She glanced at her watch—5:45 P.M. Michael had called her from Logan Airport in Boston, just after he cleared American customs and just before he was to catch his connecting flight to Portland. They had timed it out, and he was supposed to arrive at the Inn to meet her at five o'clock. For some reason, he didn't want Sam to meet him at the ferry.

I'm glad, Sam realized. *I'm way too nervous to be standing there like some welcoming committee.* She bit at a hangnail, then forced herself to stop. She looked down at the outfit she'd chosen after trying on almost everything in her closet. Nothing had seemed right.

What do you wear when you're going to meet your birth father for the first time? she'd asked herself. *This is one occasion they don't cover in your basic fashion magazine.*

Finally she decided on the only conservative pants she owned—a pair of pale pink linen trousers that Emma had insisted she buy on one of their shopping sprees. With it she wore a matching long pink linen vest. She tied a black velvet ribbon around her neck and hung a cameo she'd found in a secondhand store from the ribbon. And although she'd tried to wear her red cowboy boots with the ensemble, she knew they were totally wrong when she'd surveyed the look in the mirror. So she'd changed to beige suede flats that she hardly ever wore. She'd even kept her makeup and hair subdued, and now that she was sitting there, nervously awaiting Michael, she wished she had on her usual faded jeans and her boots. *I probably look like an idiot,* she worried. *Like I'm trying to look like Emma, because I think Michael would like her more than he's going to like me.*

Sam stood up and paced. *Hey, I am who I am,* she told herself. *There's no guarantee I'm going to like him, either.*

"Where is he?" Sam whispered out loud, looking at her watch again. She knew that a forty-five minute delay on a trip that involved an eleven-hour transatlantic flight from Israel to Boston, connecting flight to Portland, a ferry trip to Sunset Island, and a cab ride from the ferry port to the Inn was no big thing, but she still felt like jumping out of her skin with anxiety.

Okay, she said to herself. *Go sit down and read the book.* On impulse, she had brought along the copy of *They Survived* which was the book that Michael's sister had written about her parents. But she hadn't the inclination to actually read it. So it sat on the table in front of her. Sam had already checked to see whether there might be a family portrait in it of Beth, Michael, and her biological grandparents, but there wasn't.

How out of it am I? Sam asked herself. *I didn't even ask Michael anything about his sister, and whether he plans to see her on this trip here, when I talked to him. Does that mean that I'm totally selfish?*

Sam looked around at the other people on the deck. It was a perfect Maine late afternoon—the temperature was in the high seventies, the sun was shining, and the sky was totally cloudless, with a very light breeze blowing. All around her, couples were looking romantically into each other's eyes, families were gathered for predinner drinks, local business people were sharing some after-work comradery.

One thing's for sure—I'm the only person out here who is about to meet with a man who a few days ago was in a prisoner of war camp, Sam thought. *And didn't know that I even existed. And who is my biological father. The world is just too weird for me!* She looked for the millionth time at the entrance to the back deck, but no one was coming through.

Luckily, Dan took the monsters to Portland for the afternoon. He should take them for family therapy, if he wants my opinion.

Sam opened the book, but just stared at the page, unable to concentrate.

"Oh, Sammi!" a southern-accented voice called out from afar.

Oh God, it's Lorell Courtland, Sam thought. *And if she's calling to me, then Diana can't be far behind.* Sam whirled to see where Lorell was. This time Sam's intuition was wrong. Lorell had walked out onto the deck of the Inn by herself.

Sam forced herself to put a smile on her face. It was a sour grin. "Hi, Lorell, bye Lorell," she said evenly, not wanting to get into an insult match in such a public place.

"Don't worry. I won't interfere with whatever it is you're waitin' on," Lorell assured Sam. "I just wanted to tell you that you have managed to dress decently, for once."

"Gee, thanks," Sam replied.

"It's too bad you got stood up the one time you actually look decent!"

"I didn't get stood up," Sam told her, trying to control her temper. She decided to change the subject. "What brings you here?"

Lorell smiled falsely at Sam. "Oh,

sugar," she trilled, "I'm meetin' the cutest guy from the beach here for a date. He's in medical school."

"Oh, great," Sam commented. *Yeah, like I could care less.*

"He's rich," Lorell related, a thrill in her voice.

"Cool," Sam muttered.

"And what about you?" Lorell asked. "Are you waitin' on that surfer guy, Nick?"

"Nope," Sam said, wishing Lorell would disappear. Unfortunately, Lorell seated herself at the table next to Sam.

"Diana said Nick is a jerk," Lorell stated primly.

"He's not a jerk," Sam answered, trying to keep her voice under control.

"That's not what *some* people say," Lorell said knowingly.

"Some people are wrong," Sam hissed.

Lorell smiled a beatific smile. "Well, then maybe I'll have to see for myself. So, who are you waitin' on?"

Why did she have to show up now? Sam asked herself desperately, looking toward the door every few seconds.

"A friend," Sam said tersely.

Lorell looked toward the entranceway, where Sam kept glancing. "Must be an important friend," she cooed. "You're awfully nervous."

"Yeah, well . . ." Sam replied, and then added a shrug. *Please, go away! Just go away!*

"Hum, I can't wait to get a look at this 'friend' of yours, myself," Lorell finally said. "Well, I'll just be leaving you alone, for you to wait for your friend." To Sam's great relief, Lorell got up from the table.

"You do that," Sam said.

"And maybe you'll be able to introduce me to your friend," Lorell added. "I'll be sittin' right over there, where the view of the beach is better. See you! Oh! What's that book you're reading?"

Sam fingered *They Survived.* "Uh, nothing special," she answered. She moved the book out of Lorell's way, but Lorell quickly grabbed it from her.

"It's about Jews?" Lorell asked, wrinkling her nose prettily.

"It's about survivors of the Holocaust," Sam said evenly.

"Oh that," Lorell commented dismissively.

139

"Lorell," Sam said, holding back every urge she had to stand up and toss her drink in her face, "why don't you take off now, okay?"

"Bye!" Lorell said. "I'm looking forward to seeing your friend."

Just at that moment, a ruggedly handsome guy with blond hair and a blond moustache, wearing a T-shirt that read GEORGETOWN U. MED SCHOOL and jeans came out on the back porch.

"My date," Lorell trilled, waving to the good-looking guy.

"Goody for you," Sam said, thrilled that Lorell was finally leaving.

Sam turned back to her table. *Where is he?* she said to herself. *Not that I want him to meet Lorell. What an introduction to the United States!* She forced herself to pick up *They Survived,* and she opened to the front page and tried to read. This time, for some reason, she found the narrative interesting, and managed to lose herself in her aunt's book for a few pages.

"Samantha Bridges?" a voice said to her from close by, interrupting her concentration.

Sam looked up.

Oh my God, she thought, *it's him.*

Michael Blady looked even more like Sam in real life than he did on television. His neatly trimmed hair was exactly the same color and texture as her wild red locks. Their eyes were precisely the same color of blue. And Michael had the same thin, lanky build as Sam. Sam figured that she was only a couple of inches shorter than he was. Actually, he was very, very thin, and his skin was even paler than Sam's got in the dead of winter.

They probably didn't feed him when he was a prisoner, Sam thought. *They probably kept him locked away somewhere where there was no sunlight.* Even though she barely knew Michael, that thought made her heart hurt.

"It is a miracle," Michael said simply, after Sam had identified herself to him. "May I sit?"

Sam nodded. She was actually speechless. She didn't know what to do— whether to hug this man she'd never met before, shake his hand, kiss him on the cheek, begin to tell him the story of her life, or just do nothing. So she did the easiest thing. She just did nothing.

She and Michael looked at one another without speaking, but Sam noticed a faint smile playing over Michael's lips.

"It is an uncomfortable moment, no?" he asked.

"A little," Sam admitted. *A lot,* she thought.

"For me as well as for you," Michael spoke slowly and thoughtfully. "But when my parents told me of your letter, I simply had to come to you, right away. You have no idea how much difficulty it was for me."

Sam grinned a little at Michael's slightly fractured, Israeli-accented English. "You speak English really well," she said. "Better than a lot of Americans I know."

"Also Hebrew of course, and Arabic, French, and Norwegian," Michael said. "Can I order some coffee and food? I'm starving. And can I smoke? All Israelis smoke."

"It's bad for you," Sam couldn't help saying, even though she thought she sounded like a high school health ed teacher.

"I know," Michael replied. "But I do it anyway. Isn't that strange?" He motioned to a nearby waitress, who came over and took his order for coffee and a club sandwich. Sam ordered the same.

"You speak a lot of languages," Sam said, after the waitress had left them. "Like my friend Emma."

"Emma?" Michael asked gently. "Tell me about Emma. Tell me about your friends."

Sam was puzzled. *Of all the things to ask me about, why is he asking me about my friends? We don't know anything really about each other, but he is asking me about my friends. Weird.*

That odd half-grin played across Michael's face again, laugh lines crinkling a bit around his blue eyes. "You are wondering why I am asking about your friends, right?"

Sam nodded.

"It is as good a place to begin as any," Michael said, philosophically. "Then I

143

will tell you something about me—whatever you want to know."

"Okay," Sam agreed, but she felt shy. "Well, my two best friends in the world are here on Sunset Island with me. They're really different from me, and they're really great."

And she went on to tell Michael of how she met up with Emma and Carrie, and some of the adventures they'd had. The more she talked, the easier it got. Michael was a great listener, clearly eager to hear everything about Sam's life. He kept encouraging her, enjoying every detail. She talked about her childhood in Kansas, her dream of being a performer, her brief appearance on Broadway, and even about her job on Sunset Island.

"You have a wonderful life," Michael said when Sam finished.

"I do?" Sam questioned. "Yeah, I guess I do," she added with a grin. "Sometimes I think that if it weren't for Emma and Carrie, I couldn't make it through half the stuff that comes my way."

"You are a fortunate girl to have friends like your Emma and Carrie."

I like him, Sam thought. *A lot. He hasn't spoken more than a dozen sentences to me and I can tell that I like him.* Sam watched as he bit into the club sandwich that the waitress had brought while she was speaking.

"Okay," Sam said, a little of her usual bravado returning. "Now it's my turn."

"Okay," Michael said, that wonderful smile still on his face. "I'm ready."

What I really want to know is about you and Susan, she thought. *Why doesn't she want to see you? How can she stand to stay away?* But she forced herself not to ask Michael about this . . . yet.

"How did you get captured?" she queried.

Michael sighed. "War," he said. "It is terrible."

"That is not an answer," Sam noted. "You promised—"

"And so I did," Michael continued. "I was on a mission in Lebanon. It was the early 1980s. The northern part of Israel was receiving rocket fire from terrorists."

"What happened?"

"My job was to interrogate prisoners.

145

Strange, isn't it, that I should then become a prisoner? What is the word . . . ?"

"Ironic?" Sam suggested.

"Yes, that's it," Michael agreed. "It is ironic." He lit up a cigarette and blew the smoke out. "My unit ran into an ambush. Most of us got away, but two men were wounded."

"So if you got away—"

"Four of us went back to get the wounded men," Michael explained. "A sniper killed two of us. Two of us were captured. One of us died in prisoner of war camp. One of us is here with you."

That is so amazing, Sam thought. *My father is a hero. If he hadn't gone back to the wounded men, he would have gotten clean away, and he would never have been taken prisoner—*

"Oh! Sammi!"

Lorell. No, no, please, God, make her go away.

Lorell walked toward her and Michael.

"Is this one of your friends?" Michael asked.

"Hardly," Sam replied under her breath.

"Hi, Sammi!" Lorell trilled. "Larry had

146

to go to the little boys' room, so I thought I'd come over and get introduced to your date. He is so, well, *distinguished-looking!*"

Sam knew this was Lorell's way of commenting on the fact that Michael was so much older than she was. And the last thing Sam wanted Lorell to know was the truth—that Michael Blady was her biological father. It would be just one more thing for Lorell and Diana to harp on. And frankly, it was none of her business.

"He's a friend," Sam said firmly.

"A friend?" Lorell echoed, giving Michael a piquant look.

"A friend," Michael agreed, picking up on Sam's cue.

"He speaks!" Lorell cooed. "And I notice that your friend has an accent. Charming. What did you say your name was?"

"Michael," Michael answered. "I am a friend of Sam's family."

"Is that so?" Lorell chirped. "You know, you two could be father and daughter, you look so much alike."

"Hmm, a coincidence," Michael commented.

"So, where are you from, friend Michael?" Lorell asked.

"I am from Israel," Michael said firmly. "And if you would excuse us, Sam and I are discussing some family business."

Sam was impressed. Michael was telling the truth, without exactly telling the truth. *A useful skill*, she thought.

"Oh!" Lorell said, with exaggerated politeness. "Then please, excuse me. I do have to say, Michael, you look very familiar to me. Very. Have I seen you someplace before?"

"No," Michael replied. "We've never met."

"That is so strange," Lorell commented. "I could absolutely swear that I've seen you before. Even recently!"

Oh no, Sam thought. *She's going to recognize him. Don't tell me Lorell actually watches the news.*

"Well," Lorell said, "Larry is back. I'm going to have to think about this, Michael. Because I know you. I don't know where from. But I'll think of it, never fear. Bye!"

Lorell left. Sam looked at Michael, who looked back at her.

"She is a phony," Michael stated.

Sam grinned. *I'm getting to like him more and more and more.*

TEN

"You sure you're too tired to go?" Sam asked Michael as they walked outside after dinner. "My friends want to meet you so much. And . . . I want you to meet them, too."

"I would love to meet with them," Michael said, rubbing his eyes wearily, "but I can hardly keep my eyes open now."

"I'm sorry," Sam said quickly, "I kept you for hours—"

"You did not keep me, little one," Michael corrected her. "It was my great pleasure. You are the reason I am here." He patted her gently on the shoulder.

Sam smiled, and got a warm feeling all over. "Yeah, I guess I am, at that."

Sam explained about her job, and

Michael understood that she needed to work in the morning. They planned for Sam to call him when she woke up.

"Do you want me to drive you to your hotel?" Sam asked Michael.

"No, I'll catch this taxi," he replied, cocking his head toward a cab in front of the restaurant. He took Sam's hand and smiled at her.

There are tears in his eyes, Sam realized, and she felt a lump come to her own throat.

"Sweet dreams," was all he said, and then he walked away.

Sam drove quickly over to the Play Café, and made her way through the crowd toward the group's usual table. The fraternity group that had been partying on the beach earlier in the week had discovered the place, and frat boys were chanting bawdy songs and playing drinking games. They were all over the room, making it difficult for Sam to get by. There was a momentary break in the crowd where four guys decided to sit in the middle of the floor for no apparent reason. In the clearing, Sam caught a glimpse of Carrie, who also saw her.

"Hey, Sam!" Carrie called when she saw her.

Sam waved and worked her way around the frat boys, who lustily invited her to join them.

"In your dreams," Sam shot back, but there was a grin on her face. Once she got around the frat guys, she saw that Billy and Nick were at the table with Carrie and Emma. When a huge line-backer type with a buzz haircut moved out of her way, Sam's heart turned over, because she saw that someone else was at the table, too. Presley Travis. And he was sitting next to Emma.

Sam forced herself to smile gaily as she approached the table. *He's not my boyfriend anymore,* she told herself, *so I just have to get over it. But if it turns out that he and Emma turn out to be . . .* Sam forced herself off this line of thought. It was just too awful to consider.

"We didn't know these guys were going to be here," Carrie whispered in Sam's ear. "So, where is he?"

"Exhausted," Sam explained. "He went to get some sleep."

"Can we still meet him?" Emma asked.

"Tomorrow afternoon, maybe for lunch, if you can get off," Sam told them, taking a seat next to Nick.

"What 'him' are you talking about?" Nick asked casually.

"Uh, just a friend," Sam said. She did her best not to look at Pres, or to notice how close he was sitting to Emma. She forced herself to sound light and carefree. "Cute outfit, Em," she said.

"Thanks," Emma said with a smile. Emma had on a ruffled denim shirt with a bare midriff under her white jean jacket, and white jeans.

Why does she have to look so good in that? Sam asked herself. *Why do the two of them look so good together? And why am I making something out of nothing? It has to be nothing. It just has to.*

"One super-deluxe seafood special," the waitress announced, depositing a huge pizza on the table.

"Dig in!" Billy said, reaching for a slice of pizza.

"Not hungry," Sam said honestly.

"What's the matter?" Carrie asked, totally astonished. She'd never known Sam to turn down food, much less a Play Café super-special seafood pizza, "Do you feel okay?"

"Yeah, I'm just not hungry," Sam said.

Pres put a slice of pizza on a plate and handed it to Emma.

God, he's feeding her, Sam thought miserably. *He really likes her. Damn.*

"Are you sure you're okay?" Emma asked with concern. "You really don't look very well."

"I just ate, remember?" Sam replied, almost snapping at Emma.

Emma was taken aback. "I know," she said quietly. "I just never saw you not hungry unless you were sick."

Sam felt instantly contrite. "I'm sorry. I'm . . . I've just got stuff on my mind."

"Like this mystery guy you were just with?" Nick asked, biting into his pizza.

All of a sudden, Sam felt exhausted. It was all just too much, too overwhelming. She didn't care who knew about Michael Blady, and she didn't care what they thought.

"The mystery guy I was just with is my father."

All the guys stopped eating.

"My birth father," Sam added. And she quickly told them the whole story.

Pres looked both fascinated and astonished.

Well, no wonder he's so interested, Sam thought. *It's not because of me. It's because he's adopted too, and he's been trying to find his birth parents for a long time.*

"Wow, what a trip," Nick commented, reaching for another slice of pizza.

Pres shook his head. "Girl, I can't believe you didn't tell me he was coming."

"Why should I?" Sam asked belligerently.

Pres looked hurt. "Well, I kind of thought this adoption thing was something we shared. . . ."

"Maybe you forgot," Sam said pointedly. "We don't share anything anymore."

Pres gave her a steady look. "We share friendship, Sam," he said evenly. "At least I thought we did."

Then Sam saw Pres edge his chair closer to Emma's, lean over, and whisper something in Emma's ear. She saw Emma nod thoughtfully, and then nod again.

I wonder what that's all about, Sam

thought miserably. *Correction, I'm sure I know what that's all about. It's about me not telling him.*

"So," Carrie prompted her, "tell us what it was like."

"Yeah," Billy urged her, "this is from-the-heart stuff."

"You don't have to unless you want to," Emma added kindly.

Sam smiled at her friend. *How can I be mad at her when she's so terrific?*

Suddenly, Pres got up from the table. "Excuse me a sec," he said. "I gotta go check the lock on my bike."

"But you're always careful about that," Sam said, "and—"

"Excuse me," Pres said again, and he walked out toward the door of the Play Café.

Sam felt herself broadsided by a wave of emotion. *I've just got to talk to him, no matter what happens,* she thought to herself. *No matter what he thinks.* She got up from the table, too.

"Where are you going?" Carrie asked her.

"Uh, bathroom emergency," Sam said quickly, starting to move after Pres.

"Hurry back. We want to hear everything," Emma said.

But Sam was already on her way. She made her way to the bathroom and turned quickly to see if her friends were watching her. They weren't. So she hustled out after Pres. Maybe she could still catch him.

"Well, well," Pres drawled, "fancy meetin' you here."

Sam edged over closer to where Pres was standing, near his motorcycle that was parked in the Play Café's small parking lot.

"I told you your bike was okay," Sam said.

Pres straightened up. "Is that what you came out here to tell me?"

"No," Sam admitted.

"Well, why don't you just say what you mean for once?"

"I'm trying to," Sam answered. "You're making me nervous." She twisted a silver ring around her pinky. "Look, I'm sorry I didn't tell you about this," she finally said. "But, I mean, we haven't really been talking lately. I didn't even know if you'd care."

"I haven't stopped caring about you," Pres said in a low voice.

"You haven't?" Sam asked hopefully, her heartbeat speeding up.

"As a friend," Pres added.

"Oh, sure, I knew that was what you meant," Sam said smoothly. "I guess you're busy with Emma now—"

"C'mon Sam, grow up," Pres interrupted. "This doesn't have anything to do with Emma. You should have called me and I feel bad that you didn't. But you didn't. And only you know why."

"It's because—"

"It doesn't matter, does it?" Pres asked her. "What's done is done."

"I'm sorry," Sam said contritely. Pres stood there for a moment, not saying anything. Then, when he did speak, his voice was gentle.

"Sam," he said. "I know it isn't easy. Dang, I know better'n most anyone what you're going through. And I know you're not my girlfriend. But you gotta treat me like a friend if you want me to be a friend."

"I do!" Sam replied.

"Then start actin' that way," Pres told her. "And do yourself a favor. Steer clear of Nick."

Why's he telling me that? Sam thought. *He must be jealous. Well, that's a good sign.*

"Why?" Sam asked. "He's a nice guy."

"He's a competent drummer," Pres said, his tone even. "With a whole lot of personal problems."

"Such as?" Sam asked.

"You can either take my word for it, or find out for yourself," Pres replied. "I'm talkin' one friend to another."

"What'd he do?" Sam asked. "What is the big deal?"

"C'mon," Pres said, refusing to answer Sam's question. "They'll wonder where you are. Where'd you say you went?"

"Bathroom," Sam grinned.

"I'm headin' in," Pres said. "You coming?"

"I'll be there in a minute."

"Suit yourself," Pres said. He reached over and touched her hair gently. "Call me. If you dare. We'll talk."

"You got it, pardner," Sam replied, and Pres turned to walk back into the café.

Should I ask him? Sam questioned herself. *Oh hell, what do I have to lose anyway?*

"Hey, Pres, if we're such good friends, can I ask you something?" Sam called to him.

He turned around. "Sure."

"You interested in Emma?" Sam asked lightly. "Not that it matters or anything. I was just asking."

Pres gave Sam an odd look. "Yeah, I'm interested in her," he replied. "As a friend. As just a friend."

"Like me," Sam commented.

"That's right," Pres said, "like you."

"Becky's late," Dan Jacobs announced, as Sam let herself into the Jacobs house after having hung out at the Play Café with her friends until nearly midnight. He was sitting with Allie in the kitchen, both of them drinking glasses of milk and eating cookies. He sounded more irritated than worried.

"Yeah, she's late," Allie echoed. "I think Dad should ground her! Like forever!"

Sam pulled up a chair. "When was she supposed to be here?"

"An hour ago," Dan explained.

"Where'd she go?" Sam asked.

"With Ian," Allie snorted, as if that explained everything.

"Young love's gonna kill me," Dan commented.

"She's not in love, Dad," Allie cracked. "She's in lust."

Dan Jacobs looked shocked. "That isn't funny, young lady."

Allie rolled her eyes. "Get a grip, Dad."

"You girls are too young to . . . do whatever it is you're thinking about," Dan said.

Oh, very helpful, Sam thought to herself, reaching for the carton of milk.

"Hey, I'm only thinking," Allie said smugly. "She's the one who's out doing."

"She better not be or I'll ground her for the rest of her life," Mr. Jacobs vowed.

This guy is a lunatic, Sam thought. *One minute he's too permissive and the next minute he's suffocating them. Yuck.*

"She's in big trouble," Mr. Jacobs added.

"They took their bikes, Dad," Allie remonstrated, quickly switching to her sister's defense for the moment. "How far could they be?"

"It doesn't matter," Dan explained. "It's the principle of the thing."

"Want me to go look for her?" Sam offered. "I could take the car."

"Naah," Dad said. "She'll be here soon."

"Don't be so sure, Dad," Allie muttered.

"You know something I don't?" he asked his daughter, putting down the cookie he was eating.

"No, but she's in lust!" Allie cackled with glee.

At that moment, all three of them heard Becky letting herself into the house.

"You're in trouble!" Allie sang out, obviously changing her mind once again, this time in favor of getting her sister busted.

"Young lady, come in here," Dan ordered.

Becky walked into the kitchen. She had on a face that Sam could only describe as being a mixture of contrition and defiance. She sat down at the table.

"You're late," Dan said to her.

"Real late," Allie added.

"Please be quiet," Dan said to Allie. "In fact, get up to your room."

"But Dad—"

"Get to your room!" Dan yelled.

Whoa baby, I've never, ever heard Dan yell at either of his kids, Sam thought. *Usually he's about as forceful as a dead gerbil.*

Allie looked shocked, and she quickly got up from the table and sulked away. Dan was left with Becky and Sam.

"You're late," Dan repeated.

"I know," Becky answered, attempting an air of bravado.

"Where were you?" Dan asked.

"With Ian."

"What were you doing?"

"Riding our bikes," Becky said with exasperation.

"You had me very worried," Dan explained.

Becky put her hands on her hips. "It's not like I haven't been late before. What's the biggie?"

"The biggie is that I was concerned about you," Dan Jacobs explained. "The biggie is that I'm responsible for you—"

"So since when do you take that very seriously?" Becky snapped.

Mr. Jacobs's face drained of color. "You are grounded for a week."

Sam looked over at Becky to see how she'd react. She expected to see Becky get angry at her punishment. And for a moment, anger did cross her face. But it was quickly replaced by something close to resignation.

"Okay, Dad," Becky replied.

"Okay?" Dan asked, astonished that his daughter was actually accepting her penalty.

"That's what I said. I was late. I pay," Becky said. "Can Ian still come over?"

"I'll have to think about that," Dan answered. "Good night."

"Good night?"

"Good night."

Becky got up, her head held high, and left the room.

This is unbelievable, Sam thought. *Dan is actually punishing her, and Becky is actually accepting her punishment. Now if he'll only stand up to her on the can-Ian-come-over issue. God, I must be losing it. I'm actually in favor of an adult punishing a teenager!*

"How did I do?" Mr. Jacobs asked Sam in a shaky voice.

"Great," Sam replied honestly.

Mr. Jacobs scratched his unshaven chin and stared into the distance. "Today is . . . would have been . . . my wedding anniversary."

"Uh-huh," Sam said, since "congratulations" hardly seemed appropriate.

"I just starting thinking, how I would die if I lost one of the twins like I lost my wife." He focused back on Sam again with an abashed smile. "I guess you don't know what it's like to love someone that much yet."

"Maybe not," Sam agreed gently. She said good night and slowly made her way upstairs. But as she reached her room, she knew that there were only two people above everyone else that she really loved that much, even if they did drive her crazy sometimes. They weren't Michael Blady or Susan Briarly, and they weren't even Carrie and Emma.

They were her parents. And she hadn't even called them.

ELEVEN

"Nice shot, Sam!" Carrie yelped, as Sam rolled the wooden ball up the Skee-Ball ramp and watched it score a direct hit in the area that read "100 points."

"Talent, Carrie, pure talent," Sam replied, reaching for another ball.

"I can't believe you're playing Skee-Ball before breakfast," Carrie said, watching Sam roll the next ball for another hundred points.

"Me neither," Emma marveled. "Sam never does anything before breakfast."

"Not true," Sam replied.

"Then what?" Carrie asked.

"I sleep." She rolled another ball and scored fifty. "I say as long as the kiddies are out of our hair for a while, we should take advantage of it."

Carrie looked down to the beach where the kids that the girls took care of were at an early morning swim, courtesy of the teen summer staff of the Sunset Country Club who had planned an outing for them.

"We've got another hour," Carrie reported, looking at her watch. "Then it's back to the battlefield."

"I suggest we make the most of it," Sam said regally, reaching for another ball and rolling it up the ramp. "Bingo!"

"Another hundred points," Emma marveled. "I don't know how you do it."

"It's all in the wrist," Sam answered. "You try." She tried to hand Emma the one remaining ball in the game, but Emma shook her head.

"You're amazing," Emma said. "How can you be so cool when your birth father is asleep at a hotel on this very island, right this very minute?"

"Ice in my veins." Sam took the final ball from Emma's hand, gave an elegant wind-up, and rolled it up the Skee-Ball ramp once again. This time it landed in the semicircle that gave Sam eighty additional points.

"Four hundred forty for the game," Carrie calculated, including the score she had racked up earlier. "That gives you a giant panda!"

"Lady," the guy who was running the Skee-Ball game said, "you ought to think about turning pro." He reached up to a big rack and pulled down a giant stuffed panda, and handed it to Sam.

Sam made her forefinger and her thumb into the shape of a gun, and blew mock smoke away from the tip of her forefinger. "Turn pro? I coach the pros," she said superciliously. Her friends cracked up. Sam gave her giant panda a big kiss. "I'm naming this one Danny."

"You would," Emma grinned. "He's cute enough."

"Have you called him?" Carrie asked, leaning against a railing.

"Who?" Sam asked absentmindedly, lifting her face up to the sun.

"Danny, obviously, " Carrie said. "Have you called him to tell him about Michael?"

"Well, not exactly," Sam said slowly.

"So did you call your parents in Kansas?" Emma queried.

169

Sam danced her new Danny panda on her leg. "Uh, I've been thinking about it. . . ."

Carrie peered at Sam. "Hold the phone. Are you telling us that you're out here la-de-da playing Skee-Ball, and you haven't even called your parents and told them what's going on?"

"Well, they're pretty busy in the summer," Sam began.

"Sam!" Emma exclaimed. "That's ridiculous!"

Sam's face fell. "I know," she admitted. "I'm acting crazy! But every time I think about picking up the phone to call them, I break out in a cold sweat!"

"How come?" Emma asked.

"I don't know!" Sam cried with irritation. "If I was bright enough to know maybe I would have called them by now! Come on, let's take a walk."

The threesome strolled down the boardwalk, stuffed Danny dangling by his wrist from Sam's hand. Sam saw a young girl with red hair happily walking with her parents, one of them holding her right hand, one of them holding her left. It filled her with guilt.

"Don't bite my head off," Carrie began, "but is it that you're afraid your parents will feel hurt if they know about Michael?"

Sam sighed heavily. "No, not hurt so much as . . . threatened. That's it. Threatened. It's been bad enough with Susan, but now this! Why should I put myself through it?"

"But how can you avoid it?" Emma wondered.

"Well, I've done a pretty good job so far," Sam said dryly.

"I think you're being really hard on yourself," Carrie started loyally. "Maybe you're trying to protect them."

"And maybe I'm just trying to protect myself," Sam replied. She felt irritable and anxious, and she wanted to drop the whole subject. "How about some breakfast? I'm starved from all this exertion."

They made their way to one of the many outdoor self-service restaurants that lined the boardwalk. Once they got their food, they took it to one of the white wooden tables and sat down to eat.

"When did Michael say he was going to

meet you again?" Carrie asked Sam as she took a big gulp of orange juice.

"I called the Inn right after I woke up," Sam explained, "and he'd actually left a message for me, telling me that I should leave a message for him."

"So?" Emma asked eagerly, sipping her tea. "Did you?"

"Of course, Boston baroness," Sam answered. "I said he should meet me and my two best friends for lunch at the Sunset Country Club at twelve-thirty."

"But you didn't ask us first!" Emma protested.

"True, I just hoped," Sam replied. She dug into her food—a plate of scrambled eggs, hash browns, bacon, buttered rye toast, with a slice of cantaloupe on the side.

"I'll find a way," Emma assured Sam. "I just want to make sure that you want him to meet us. Don't feel obligated or anything."

Sam laughed. "Who was I going to ask? Diana? Of course I want him to meet you! You're my best friends in the whole world. He's already asked about you."

"He has?" Carrie queried, biting into her English muffin.

"Yeah," Sam said. "I didn't get a chance to tell you last night. We talked a lot about you."

"That's nice," Emma said with a shy smile.

"You're gonna like him," Sam assured them. "My biggest worry is keeping Diana away from him."

"Why's that?" Carrie asked.

"You know Diana," Sam sighed. "She'll go after anyone if she thinks it'll make my life miserable."

"Come on," Carrie said reasonably. "It's not that bad."

"It is too that bad. You just have a hard time believing anyone is as evil as she is," Sam answered. "Hey, I'm surprised she hasn't made a play for Danny Franklin yet."

"It's only because she doesn't know him," Emma put in.

"Speaking of Danny—real Danny, not stuffed Danny," Carrie said, "you really should call him—after you call your parents."

"Yes, Ma," Sam said, a little mockingly,

but she winked to let Emma know it was all in fun.

"Well, well, well," said a female voice, approaching them from the broadwalk. "If it isn't the three oldest virgins in the state of Maine!"

Sam recognized the voice. Diana De Witt. *Leave it to Diana to ruin what is so far a pretty good day,* she thought. She turned to face her nemesis—and had an unexpected shock.

Diana was dripping wet in a white thong bikini, which more than showed off her perfectly-aerobicized body. And her arm was linked through the arm of none other than the newest member of Flirting With Danger, Nick Trenton. Nick was dripping wet, too, and was wearing only a pair of black lycra biker shorts.

Why, he's a two-timing piece of—

"It's so nice to take a dip in the ocean after a passionate night with me, don't you think?" Diana trilled, leaning into Nick.

Nick just shrugged and grinned.

"The thought of a passionate night

174

with you is enough to make me hurl, actually," Sam hissed.

Diana laughed. "Not you, silly. Nicky, here. I bet you'd like to know just how a drummer can use his hands—minus the drumsticks, of course."

"I couldn't care less," Sam managed, attempting a blasé tone.

"Oh, yes you could," Diana corrected slyly. "But you never will know, because a tease like you will never please!"

Sam got to her feet. "Why you little bi—"

"Easy, Sam," Carrie cautioned in a low voice. "She's just pressing your buttons."

"Hey," Diana protested, wrapping her arm around Nick's waist. "I'm just reporting the conventional wisdom. The gospel according to Nick, so to speak."

Sam looked at Nick. He just grinned, and shrugged again.

"You don't have much to say for yourself, do you?" Sam finally said to Nick.

"You two seem to be covering all the bases," Nick said cheerfully.

How could I ever have liked him? Sam wondered, now disgusted at the sight of him. *And how could I have confided in him?!*

Carrie stood up next to Sam. "Diana, I have a great idea. Why don't you two go swim across to Europe?"

"Is that what you want too, Sammi?" Diana said sweetly. "Because all you had to do is ask. Come on, Nick. We've got a better place to go. And I bet it's still *warm* there."

Diana turned around, leading Nick in the other direction. But she couldn't resist one more nasty comment. So she turned her head around and looked directly at Sam.

"Maybe you ought to interview us about last night, Sam," she suggested. "Maybe you'll learn something!"

"She is a bitch on wheels," Sam seethed three hours later in the main dining room of the Sunset Country Club. Michael Blady would be joining her, Emma, and Carrie any minute. Then they'd have an hour or so to be together before it was time to pick up their kids from a club cookout.

"Who, Diana?" Emma asked.

"Who else?" Sam replied.

"Let's not talk about her," Carrie suggested. "It's such a waste of time and energy."

"I can't believe she's sleeping with him," Sam groused, unable to let the subject drop. She broke off one of the breadsticks that was on the table and crammed it into her mouth.

"Why not?" Carrie replied. "She sleeps with everyone else."

"I guess," Sam answered. "I guess I can't believe he's sleeping with her!"

"Why not?" Carrie repeated. "He's not attached."

"But—"

"Sam," Emma said gently, "just because you're interested in someone doesn't mean he has to be interested in you."

"Bull," Sam snorted. "That guy was all over me!"

"Well, maybe it's for the best. Billy told me he's a jerk," Carrie reasoned. "Maybe she'll get a disease."

"Maybe he'll get a disease," Emma said emphatically, and all three friends laughed. "Maybe they deserve each other."

I don't know why I should be surprised, Sam thought to herself. *Pres said he was a cockroach. Diana sleeps with anything that zips at the crotch, particularly if she thinks it will annoy me. So she picks Nick. And it annoys me. I thought he was interested in me! But obviously he's not worth it.*

"Pres told me to watch my butt around him," Sam related. "I can't tell a lie. Remember when I was going to the bathroom last night?"

"You followed Pres," Carrie said kindly. "We know. We saw."

"But you didn't let on when I came back!" Sam exclaimed.

"Of course not," Emma said with a smile.

Sam shook her head. "You guys are too much." She looked at her watch. "He should be here any minute." She looked down at herself. "You think I look okay?"

Sam had decided that today she'd dress like her normal self. She had on faded jeans and a skinny red crocheted top that ended just above her naval. And, of course, her red cowboy boots.

"You look fabulous," Carrie assured her.

"Good morning," a deep accented male voice said, approaching the table.

Sam turned to smile at Michael. He was dressed in sneakers, a pair of blue jeans, and an open-necked white collarless shirt. He looked much less haggard than he had the night before.

Sam jumped to her feet and Michael embraced her gently. She found herself hugging him back. Emma and Carrie rose politely.

"This is Emma Cresswell," Sam said to Michael, "and this is Carrie Alden." Michael reached out to shake their hands.

"Sit down, sit down," he said quickly. "I'm not a government official or anything!" All four of them sat down, Michael taking the empty seat that was next to Sam's.

"I slept like a baby," Michael continued with a happy smile. "That inn is much more comfortable than prison."

"I bet the food's better, too," Sam said.

"She wins her bet," Michael grinned, winking at Carrie and Emma.

"So, when do we eat?" Michael asked.

Carrie laughed. "You sound just like Sam!"

Michael smiled at his daughter. "Good," he said sincerely.

"We eat now," Sam answered quickly. "There's a buffet table over there." She cocked her head toward the far wall of the dining room.

"She has a hollow leg," Carrie confided to Michael.

"That's exactly what my parents used to say about me," Michael said.

The four of them took their plates and went to the buffet. And even Sam, who had a prodigious appetite, had to stare in amazement as Michael filled his plate high with mostly fruits and vegetables, although he did take several slices of broiled turkey breast too.

"Prison camp," Michael said, when they finally got back to the table and sat down, indicating his place. "Not much fruit. Not much vegetables. I missed them. So girls, I have heard much about you two."

"I lied," Sam joked. "None of the good things are true."

"So," Michael said, "Sam told me that you all went out to California together to meet Sam's mother."

Gulp. I wasn't expecting him to bring that subject up right now. And he doesn't even look worried about raising it, Sam thought. *Maybe several years in a prisoner of war camp changes your perspective on things.*

Sam looked over at her friends. From the expressions on their faces, Michael's reference to Susan Briarly took them by surprise, too.

Emma recovered her composure the quickest. "She was very nice to us," she said, diplomatically. "A wonderful hostess."

"She is a wonderful person," Michael replied, a wistful look in his eyes. "She was a wonderful . . . no, she still must be."

"She's kind of an old hippie," Carrie mentioned, looking for something to say. Then she realized how awful that must sound. "I mean, she's not old—"

"And I'm kind of an old soldier,"

Michael replied with a shrug. "Did she ever tell you how we met?"

All three girls shook their heads no.

"Then I will tell you," Michael replied, chewing thoughtfully on a slice of avocado. "I was already in the Army— everyone in Israel serves, even the girls—wearing my uniform and carrying my Uzi submachine gun. I was on duty at the Wailing Wall in Jerusalem and she approached me, asking for directions. It was love at first sight," he said.

"That's a great story," Emma said.

"It's not the total truth," a female voice said, approaching them.

Sam whirled to face the voice.

There, in the dining room of the Sunset Country Club, looking on at the table where Sam and her friends and her birth father were sitting, was a slightly plump, short, middle-aged woman in a simple, long cotton skirt and jean jacket. It was Sam's birth mother, Susan Briarly.

TWELVE

"Susan?" Sam whispered.

"Hello," Susan replied. But she wasn't looking at Sam. She was looking at Michael.

Sam and Michael both stood up, and Sam watched her birth parents staring at each other.

"You came," Michael finally said.

"Yes," Susan said.

Michael's eyes were filled with a million things—happiness, sadness, love. "You look exactly the same," he finally murmured.

"No," Susan protested. "But you do."

The waiter got Susan a chair, and everyone sat back down. And although the group made small talk for a few minutes, it was clearly ridiculous. Michael and Susan couldn't take their eyes off each other.

Sam saw Emma give Carrie an almost imperceptible signal with her eyes.

"Uh, I think I'd better go check on Ethan and Wills," Emma announced.

"And I told Ian I'd bring him his baseball mitt," Carrie chimed in. "It's out in the car."

"Please don't go," Susan said politely.

"Please," Michael added.

I love Carrie and Emma, Sam thought. *They're so considerate. They want to give me a chance to be alone with Michael and Susan.*

"Tell you what," Sam said, "I know you've got to get back to work. How about we all meet tonight, on the beach, nine o'clock? Down by Fisherman's Jetty." Sam was referring to a semicircular rock jetty that curved out from the shoreline of the main beach.

"You got it," Carrie said. Emma nodded agreement, too. Then they were gone, and Sam was left at the table with Michael Blady on her right and Susan Briarly on her left. Her birth parents. Reunited for the first time in nineteen years.

Life is the weirdest, Sam thought. *Totally the weirdest. How did I find myself in this position?*

"Nu?" Michael said, looking first at Sam and then at Susan. Susan cracked up. Sam looked at her birth father uncomprehending. Both Susan and Michael quickly realized that she didn't get it.

"It's a Yiddish expression," Susan explained. "Yiddish is sort of a combination of Hebrew and German."

"Old people use it a lot," Michael said. "It basically means, 'so?'."

"Nu," Sam repeated, trying the expression on for size. Then she turned to Susan. "So, *nu,*" she said, "you have some explaining to do."

"You're right," Susan acknowledged, reaching for Carrie's abandoned water glass and draining it.

"Why didn't you tell me you were coming?" Sam asked her directly. "Do you think this is fair?"

Susan ignored the second part of her question. "I didn't decide to come until the last minute," she explained.

"Obviously," Sam said. "Last time I talked to you, you said you weren't going to contact Michael." Sam looked meaningfully at Michael, but Michael showed no reaction to this statement. "Now you're here. How'd you find out he was here anyway?"

"I called Joseph and Lillian in Jerusalem," Susan admitted.

"You still remember your Hebrew," Michael observed with a smile.

"Some," Susan smiled back. "Enough. They told me Michael had gone to someplace called Sunset Island in America to see Sam."

"A born spy," Michael commented, his smile broadening.

"I don't know about that," Susan grinned back. "Maybe I learned from you."

Oh God. They haven't seen each other in nineteen years, Sam thought. *They're together for all of five minutes, and they're already flirting with each other.* Then Sam laughed out loud. *I can see where I get it from. It's genetic!*

"I'm not a very good example," Michael said. "I was captured."

"So, what do you think of our daughter?" Susan asked, pride shining in her eyes.

"Smart, like you," Michael answered. "Beautiful, like you. Funny, like you."

Susan is not beautiful, Sam thought. *She's not even pretty. But he obviously still thinks she is. That's amazing. That's love, isn't it?*

"But she looks just like you," Susan noted, as she nibbled on one of the breadsticks.

"And she has a hollow leg, I'm told," Michael said. He grinned at Sam. "She's a *shayna maidel.*"

"Say what?" Sam asked.

"Pretty girl," Susan translated.

"Uh, about the Jewish thing," Sam said, searching for words, "I don't really know that much about it."

"That's okay," Michael replied. "I don't really know that much about you. We'll learn."

We'll learn. That seems to sum it right up, Sam thought to herself. *We've got so much to learn about each other. And I have so much to learn about myself. Oh God. What are my parents in Kansas*

*going to think? And when am I going to
have the courage to tell them?*

"I'm glad you were willing to talk to
me," Sam said to Pres, as the two of them
sat out together on the big wooden swing
behind the Jacobses' house. It was just
before dinner that same day. Sam was
drinking a can of diet Coke, while Pres
had a bottle of Mexican beer which Dan
Jacobs had offered him when he arrived.
There had been plenty of titters from
Allie and Becky, who had been sure that
Sam and Pres were no longer speaking to
each other. Sam had managed to persuade Dan to give her a half-hour's freedom in the backyard with Pres, pleading
she had something very important to
discuss with him.

"Hey I told you," Pres answered, taking a slow swig of his beer, "I'm your
friend if you want me to be."

"I want you to be," Sam said honestly.

After Sam told him of the day's events,
the two of them swung in silence for a
while. Sam had felt the strongest urge to
reach up and caress Pres's gorgeous long
hair, but managed to suppress it. In fact,

the two of them were barely touching at the thighs.

"That's some story you just told me," Pres finally said.

"I swear it's all true," Sam pledged, holding her fingers up in the Girl Scout salute.

Pres laughed. "I don't doubt it. It's just some story. It should be a novel."

"I can't even finish a letter," Sam lamented, "so no way I'm tackling a novel."

"Maybe I'll write it," Pres mused.

"You?" Sam asked.

"Hey, I did get me something of an education," he replied, deliberately fracturing his English, "even if it was in Tennessee. We do learn to read and write down there, contrary to what some unenlightened people think."

"I just didn't know you wrote."

"I write songs," Pres replied with a shrug. "A novel's a long song. A very long song. Anyway, I've written some short stories already."

"I didn't know that!" Sam said, amazed.

"You never asked," Pres replied dryly. "You were too busy flirting with me."

"That's not true!" Sam protested.

"Yes, it is," Pres said softly.

"Guilty as charged," Sam grinned. "But you were worth it."

"I am worth it," Pres responded. "But we'll talk about that later. Tell me more about Michael and Susan. I'm jealous. I can't even find my birth parents."

"It's weird," Sam said thoughtfully. "Really weird."

"How's that?"

"The more I know about myself, the more mixed-up I am," Sam said, searching for the right words. "It's like . . . everything I am, I'm not."

"What do you mean?" Pres asked.

"Well, I'm Christian, but I'm Jewish, I'm American, but I'm part Israeli— actually part Norwegian," Sam corrected herself. "I have two sets of parents who really don't know each other, and only one set that is married, but the parents who aren't married to each other and haven't lived together for nineteen years may be more in love than the ones who have!"

"Nice speech," Pres grinned. "I see what you mean."

"So I'm all mixed-up," Sam admitted.

"Sam," Pres said quietly, "it makes me feel really good to hear you say that."

"Why?"

"Because you're finally comin' clean with yourself, that's why," Pres said firmly. "And it's about time."

"Then if I'm doing so good, why am I feeling so bad?"

"You didn't say you were feelin' bad," Pres reminded her. "You said you were mixed-up."

"That's true," Sam replied with a rueful smile.

"Who wouldn't be?" Pres asked her. "You're human. A stone fox, I grant you, but human."

Sam grinned. "You think I'm cute?"

"Shoot, that ain't news, girl," Pres drawled.

"So—"

"So I say it's okay to be confused," Pres continued.

"I was asking about how you think I'm cute," Sam pressed.

"Sam, let's move on, okay?"

"You got it, bubba," she teased. She felt the desire again to touch him, and she fought it. *Not the right time, not the right place.*

"I've got to get going," Pres said quietly, looking at his watch. "You'll be okay?"

"Hey, I'm always okay," Sam replied breezily.

Pres gave her a look. "You ain't playing that ole tune anymore, remember?"

"Yeah," Sam replied. "Got ya."

"When you going to call the folks in Kansas?"

"Why does everyone keep asking me that?" Sam groaned.

"Because everyone is showin' a whole lot more sense than you," Pres replied archly. His eyes softened. "Maybe they'll take it better than you think," he added gently.

"Oh yeah," Sam said sarcastically. "Guess what, Vernon and Carla? I had lunch today with my birth mother and my birth father, and guess what again? My father's a war hero. So, how's the bowling team doing?"

Pres looked at Sam closely. "Don't underestimate your parents in Kansas," he cautioned. "After all, they adopted you."

* * *

After dinner with Allie and Becky (Dan was having dinner with a "lady friend," as he put it)—an excruciating affair where Allie and Becky made kissing noises at Sam every few minutes—Sam gave a small sigh of relief. Dan was due home early, and she had the evening free, until nine o'clock when she was going to join her friends and her birth parents on the beach.

On her way upstairs to shower, a wave of guilt washed over Sam. *No, first I've got to call my parents,* she thought. *It's the right thing to do. I have to call them now. I can't put it off anymore.*

She sat on her bed and dialed her home number, and to her great relief there was no answer.

Okay, that's that, Sam said to herself, hanging up the phone. *No one can say I didn't try.*

Then, before she could change her mind, she took out a piece of paper and a pen and sat down at her tiny desk to write.

It was a letter to Michael's parents in Israel—and Sam remembered that it had been a letter from her to them that had set this whole amazing chain of events off in the first place.

Dear Joseph and Lillian,

I've met Michael. In fact, Michael and Susan and I all had lunch together today, and we are all going to the beach together tonight. Along with my best friends. Do you have good beaches in Israel? Michael says you do.

Now that I've met your son—my birth father—I am prouder than ever to be a part of your family. I am proud that you are my grandparents. I'm totally confused, of course, because I already have parents and grandparents. But that's okay. Maybe I'll get less confused as I get older. I hope!

I look forward to the day when we can meet, and Michael can be our translator. In any case, I already know two very important words of Hebrew.

Shalom and L'Chaim!
Peace and to life!

Sam (Samantha) Bridges

Sam looked over what she'd written, and got a terrible feeling in the pit of her stomach.

Guilt, she realized. *That's it. I feel guilty. I feel like I'm being disloyal to my real parents, just by writing this letter.*

Why does it have to be so hard?

THIRTEEN

Sam brushed her hair and put the finishing touches on her makeup. She glanced at the clock on her nightstand—8:15. She still had time to try to call her parents in Kansas before she went to the beach to meet everyone. But just as she was crossing to the phone, it rang.

"Hello?"

"Hi, it's Susan."

"Oh, hi," Sam said, sitting on her bed. "I didn't expect to hear from you—I mean, I'm seeing you in, like, forty-five minutes, right?"

"Right," came Susan's voice. "But I didn't think we'd get any time alone, and I thought I owed you more of an explanation than you got today."

"Okay," Sam said, listening intently.

"I . . . this is very difficult for me," Susan said in a faltering voice. "I guess it isn't news to you that Carson and I are having some difficulties in our marriage."

"You told me that," Sam reminded her.

"Yes, well, I wasn't completely honest when I said they had nothing to do with you or with Michael. Carson is threatened by the fact that you exist. And no matter how much I reassure him, it doesn't seem to help."

Sam gulped hard. "I never meant to make trouble for you. . . ."

"Oh, Sam, please don't think that!" Susan cried. "I've tried to tell myself for a long time that Carson and I could work out our problems, but maybe I've been lying to myself. We weren't getting along very well before you ever contacted me."

"Are you just saying that to make me feel better?" Sam asked.

"No, I'm telling you the truth. Carson and I had a huge fight. He went so far as to forbid me to come here, to see you or Michael," Susan continued earnestly. "Well, it was ridiculous. First of all, no one 'forbids' me from doing anything. And you can't hide from your heart."

"I'm not sure I know what you mean," Sam said softly.

"Sam, I love you. You are my daughter. If Carson can't accept that, then I can't accept Carson."

"But . . . but I don't want that kind of responsibility!" Sam cried.

"Oh, honey, I'm messing this all up," Susan said with a sigh. "It's not your responsibility. I think I've been trying to convince myself for years now that Carson and I have a good marriage, but it isn't true. And then when I saw Michael again . . ."

"Do you still love him?"

"I don't know," Susan said honestly. "I've messed up a lot of things in my life. And the time I shared with him was a very long time ago. But . . . we spent some time together last night, after you left. And . . . well, let's just say I still care about him. Very much. And he cares about me."

"Wow," Sam breathed.

"Yeah, wow is right," Susan agreed.

"Michael wants me to come to Israel to visit him."

"Are you going to go?" Sam asked.

"I don't know yet," Susan replied. "I have to give it a lot of thought. Adam is on his own now, but as you know Carson and I have a baby to consider in all this."

"It's complicated," Sam agreed.

"No kidding," Susan said with a quick, rueful laugh. "Well, I just wanted to tell you this. I didn't want to leave you out."

"Thanks," Sam said sincerely. "I mean it."

"You are the greatest daughter," Susan said. "I just want you to know."

Sam hung up and stared into the distance for a moment, lost in thought. *The greatest daughter. I feel funny when she says that. I'm her daughter, but I'm not her daughter.* She reached over and quickly picked up the phone, dialing her home number.

"Hello?"

"Mom? It's me," Sam said, clutching the phone hard in her hand.

"Oh, Sam!" her mother cried happily. "Hi, honey. Dad and I were just saying we needed to call you!"

"Why?" Sam asked. *Do they already know?*

"Well, just to catch up, honey," her mother said sweetly. "How's my girl?"

She doesn't know, Sam realized. My mother is incapable of subterfuge.

"I'm good, Ma," Sam said. "Is Daddy there?"

"Yes, he's in the living room reading the paper. Want to talk to him?"

"Actually, I want to talk with both of you," Sam told her mother.

"Are you okay?" Mrs. Bridges asked quickly, a note of concern in her voice.

"I'm fine, honest," Sam replied.

"Vernon!" Sam heard her mother cry. "Pick up the extension. Sam's on the phone!"

Sam heard a click on the line.

"Sam?" came her father's deep voice.

"Hi, Daddy," Sam said warmly.

"Well, hi there. How are you?"

"I'm good," Sam said. "How's everyone?"

"Ruth Ann has a cold, but otherwise everything is fine," her father said.

"Remember your friend Jackie Laramie from high school?" her mother said. "She got married at the church last Sunday. It was lovely."

"That's nice," Sam said, her heart pounding in her chest. "Have . . . have the two of you watched the news lately?"

"We try to catch it in the evenings," her mother said. "Why? Are you that famous?"

Sam smiled. "Not yet, Mom. Do you remember seeing a story about Israeli soldiers being held as prisoners in Lebanon?"

"I caught that," Sam's dad said. "Brave men, I'd say."

"Yeah," Sam agreed. "Well, do you remember hearing how one more Israeli prisoner came back than they expected in the exchange?"

"I do, dear," her mom said. "I saw his photo in the paper, but I didn't catch his name. I remember thinking, Why, if he doesn't look like . . ." her mother's voice trailed off.

"Mom? Are you there?"

There was a beat of silence. "We're here, dear," her mother said tremulously.

"His name is Michael Blady, Mom. The

same name in the space for 'father' on my birth certificate."

More silence.

"He . . . he's your father," Sam's dad said.

"He's my *birth* father," Sam amended. "He's here on the island right now. He came to meet me."

"Goodness!" Sam's mother said. "Well, I . . . I don't know quite what to say."

"Susan is here, too," Sam continued, figuring she might as well tell them everything.

"Well, I guess your father is a big hero," Sam's dad finally said. "It's kind of hard to compete with that!"

Sam closed her eyes with pain. *This is just what I was afraid of,* she thought miserably. *That they'd be threatened. Anger flared in the pit of her stomach. If they'd just told me I was adopted when I was a kid instead of hiding it from me we wouldn't be in this stupid position!*

"Look, I didn't call to tell you so that you'd feel bad," Sam explained patiently. "I just thought you should know."

"Is he a nice man?" Sam's mother asked in a small voice.

"He's okay," Sam said tersely, not wanting to make her parents feel any worse by going on about how great Michael was.

"You sound angry, Samantha," her father pointed out.

Sam sighed. "I didn't mean to . . ."

"But you still are," her father said sadly. "You still haven't forgiven us for not telling you that you're adopted."

"I have," Sam insisted. "I . . . I just have all these crazy, mixed-up feelings. Half the time I don't understand them myself."

"Why don't you explain how you feel," her mother suggested.

"No, it's cool. I'm okay. It doesn't matter," Sam insisted, pacing nervously with the phone.

And then she heard a voice in her head. A voice with a sexy, southern accent: *"You're finally comin' clean with yourself."* That's what Pres said.

"Look, that's a total lie," Sam blurted out. "It does matter. I am still angry with you. I feel guilty about that. I feel guilty about everything! I feel like I'm being disloyal to you if I even like Michael and

Susan, and then I feel even more angry that you make me feel that way!"

"Seems to me you're doing it to yourself, young lady," her father said in a cold voice.

"Maybe," Sam agreed. "But maybe you two need to own up to how threatened you really feel, how threatened you've always felt that I'm not your birth child. That's why you never told me I was adopted, isn't it? Maybe we all need to come clean!"

Silence greeted Sam's outburst. She was scared to hear their reaction.

"Maybe you're right," Sam's mother finally said. "Vernon?"

"Maybe," Sam's father agreed in a strained voice.

"So, we'll talk about this more sometime, right?" Sam asked them.

"We will," her mother agreed.

"Daddy?"

Her father cleared his throat. "Am I still your daddy?"

Tears sprang to Sam's eyes. "That's exactly what I mean! I feel like I have to reassure you guys all the time, and it breaks my heart!" Sam cried. "You raised me. Don't you two know that you are the only real mother and father I will ever have?"

"Are you sure?" Sam's mom asked.

"That's what she wants us to stop doing, Carla," Sam's dad said to his wife.

"Oh, my, life can be complicated, can't it?" Sam's mother said, sounding as if she was laughing through her tears.

"You are my parents, forever," Sam said in a whisper. "I love you. We'll talk more soon, okay?"

They all agreed they would, and Sam hung up, completely drained. She saw her own reflection in the mirror on her dresser, and thought she looked white as a sheet. She stuck her tongue out at herself. *Yeah, so if you're learning to be so mature and everything, why do you do the right thing and still feel like dog-meat?*

"I wish you didn't have to go," Sam told Michael as she strolled slowly down the beach with him and Susan an hour later. Emma and Carrie had suggested that Sam might want to spend some time alone with her parents on Michael's last evening in America, and they were waiting for her down the beach. It was a beautiful evening, cool and clear with a zillion stars in the sky.

"The army will send a platoon to get me if I do not return quickly," Michael said. "It is amazing they have been able to keep up the fiction that I'm there while I'm here."

"Not so amazing," Susan said. "We're talking about the Israeli army here."

Michael grinned at Susan. "That's true. They did me a big favor. And since everyone assumes I'm there, no one has recognized me here."

"I'm glad," Sam said quietly. "I would have hated that." She laughed. "That's pretty funny, coming from me, since I'm determined to become rich and famous one day!"

Michael draped his arm over Sam's shoulder. "I believe that you will, Sam. You are very special."

Susan smiled luminously at Michael. "She is, isn't she? We did good work."

Sam got that funny feeling again. "My parents did good work," she couldn't help saying. "They raised me. You two gave me up."

Michael stopped walking and turned around to face Sam. "I did not know you existed," he said earnestly. "If I had known, I would have moved heaven and earth to keep you."

Something clutched at Sam's heart. "Really?" she asked in a small voice.

"Really," Michael insisted. "If Susan would not come, I would have brought you to Israel, myself."

Sam was stunned. "You mean, I would have been an Israeli?"

"A *sabra*," Michael said fervently. "A woman raised in Israel."

"Wow," Sam breathed, thinking how exotic that sounded. "Nah, it wouldn't have worked out. You guys don't have shopping malls."

Susan and Michael laughed, and it broke the tension.

"I want you both to know that I'm sorry," Susan said. "I'm sorry that I didn't tell you, Michael, that I was pregnant with our child. I was wrong. But . . . I did what I thought was the best thing at the time."

"We cannot go back," Michael said gently. "Now, we must go forward." He turned to Sam. "I would like you to come to Israel soon, Samantha, to meet your grandparents. . . . And so I can get to know you better."

"Well, I have a job. . . ." Sam began.

"Yes, I understand," Michael agreed. "But in the fall? Or as soon as you can. I would be happy to pay for your plane ticket."

"I'd love to," Sam said happily.

Michael turned to Susan. "And I extend the same invitation to you," he said softly.

Susan stared into Michael's eyes.

"This isn't the end for us," he said softly. "You know that."

"Yes," Susan whispered. "I know."

My God, they really are still in love with each other! Sam realized. *They really and truly are!*

Just at that moment an all too familiar voice rang out in the night air.

"Sammi! Oh, Sammi!" Lorell came running over to them.

"Gee, hi, Lorell," Sam said in a flat voice.

"I was just with my new sweetie up on the boardwalk—Diana's up there with Nick, by the way—and I saw you strolling down here with your 'friends,'" she said demurely.

"Gee, great," Sam said. "Well, I guess you have to be running along. . . ."

Lorell ignored her. "And who is this?" she asked, looking Susan over.

"A friend of my friend's," Sam said with a sigh. Susan raised her eyebrows but didn't say anything.

Lorell giggled. "You just love bein' mysterious. But I had to run on over here, because I finally figured out where I know your handsome friend here from!"

Oh just great, Sam thought with a groan. *Leave it to Lorell to be the one person who recognizes him. Now it'll be all over the island. They'll make my life into a circus.*

"You can't fool me," Lorell said, waggling her finger at Michael. "You're that Brazilian movie star, the one who does all those kick-boxing movies! I even recognized your accent! I saw your picture in *The Globe* and I never forget a handsome face! What I want to know is, how do you know Sam?"

Michael choked back his laughter. "Well, you have found me out," he said gravely. "I know Sam because I am planning to use her in my next film."

"No!" Lorell breathed.

Michael nodded solemnly. "And this woman here is Arushka Gonzalez—a very famous star in my country. She will be playing Sam's mother in the movie."

Lorell cocked her head to the side. "Are you sure?" she asked, beginning to sound dubious.

"You know, in a certain light you look like a young Conchita Gomez—she is the most beautiful star in all of South America!" Michael told Lorell.

"Oh, I think I've heard of her!" Lorell said eagerly. "Well, I have been thinking about getting into show business."

"Good," Michael said. "You keep thinking. But for now, the three of us must continue to discuss our movie."

"Oh, I understand," Lorell agreed, nodding. She looked over Sam with a new respect in her eyes. "Well, I'll be toddling along. Bye, Sammi!"

As soon as Lorell was out of earshot, Sam laughed so hard she actually fell on the sand. "I can't believe you did that!" she cried, wiping the tears of laughter from her eyes. "That was absolutely the best thing I ever heard in my life!"

"I take it you don't like her," Susan said, dropping down onto the sand next to her daughter.

"I loathe her!" Sam exclaimed, still laughing. "God, you really could be a movie star!" Sam told Michael. "That was the best! Wait 'till I tell my friends! Hey, being able to shoot the bull must be genetic!"

Michael, sat down next to them. "I couldn't help myself," he admitted.

Sam grinned at him. "Don't worry about it. That stuff happens to me all the time!"

"So," Michael said, "what sort of plans do you have for yourself now, little one?"

The instant he said that, Pres's face sprang into Sam's mind. *I want him back,* she realized. *I want him back so much.*

"Well," Sam said slowly, "there's a certain person I need to come clean with."

"A boy?" Susan guessed.

Sam nodded, staring out at the sea.

"That's good, Sam," Susan said. "Don't lie to yourself and don't lie to him." She looked over at Sam. "I made a big mistake years ago. I didn't follow my heart."

"I don't want to make that mistake," Sam whispered.

Susan gently pushed a lock of hair off of Sam's face. "Sometimes you have to risk everything," she told Sam. "But just remember, the biggest failure is not to try at all."

"I'll remember," Sam said.

She looked out at the black sea rolling in to shore, and knew that she was going to risk everything, and try with all her heart to get Pres back. No more games. She'd have to tell Danny the truth, no more flirting with him. And no more stupid tangents like the one with Nick. It was time to grow up.

If I fail, I fail, she told herself. *But I don't want to end up like Susan. Twenty years from now, I want more than regrets and memories.*

There on the beach, with those two incredible people who loved her at her side, and her two best friends waiting for her, Sam knew her time was now.

SUNSET ISLAND MAILBOX

Dear Readers,

Kurt and Emma! Kurt and Emma! Kurt and Emma! According to my mail, you guys are really concerned about those two! Okay, they've got huge problems right now, but no one ever said they absolutely, positively had to be finished forever. Or should they? I really want to know whether or not you think these two should get back together.

A huge thanks to all of you who entered the Sunset Island contest! We got tons of wonderful entries! We do have a winner: her name is Amanda Hedleston. She'll be coming to visit me soon and her idea will be the basis of Sunset Fantasy—appearing in October. I'll keep you informed of all the latest developments. I only wish I could meet each and every one of you. I feel like I already know you from reading all of your ideas!

On a more serious note—I read a scary statistic in a recent survey of the twenty million thirteen- to seventeen-year-olds in the United States: eight million get drunk at least once a week, and seven million drink alone. I'd like to write more about this issue, so please let me know your thoughts. Do you drink? Alone? If so, why? How has it affected your life?

In other matters, my favorite name from this

week's mail—Crystal English of Humble, Texas. Doesn't she sound like a movie star? Thanks, Raina Stroh of Vancouver, Washington, for the great ideas. Angie Johnson of Madison, Minnesota, would like to see a book from a guy's point of view—what do you all think? Danielle Donnelly of Congers, New York, sent me some great Sunset Island art work, and to all of you cuties out there who sent me your photos, thanks! They're all up on a map of North America in my office. Keep 'em coming!

Well, it's back to work for <u>moi</u>. As always, it's a pleasure and an honor to have you as my readers. Remember, I answer each and every letter I receive. You guys are the greatest!

See you on the island!
Best—
Cherie Bennett

Cherie Bennett
% General Licensing Company
24 West 25th Street
New York, New York 10010.

Dear Cherie,

I just got through reading another Sunset book, and it was great. You are my favorite author. I would like to know what was the first book you ever wrote?

> *Your fan,*
> *Lisa K. Tharpe*
> *Skipperville, Alabama*

Dear Lisa,

The first novel I ever wrote is called <u>With a Face Like Mine</u>. I wrote it in college and it was published just after I graduated. It's about a thirteen-year-old girl growing up in the rural South in 1939. At the time that it was published, I didn't think of myself as a "writer." Isn't that weird? I was determined to be a singer and an actress. The only time I even mentioned that I was a published novelist was at parties, because I was insecure and I thought it would impress guys. It worked!

> Best,
> Cherie

Dear Cherie,

My best friend, Christy, got me started on your Sunset Island series about two years ago. I'm grateful because your books are great! One question I have, is Sam's birth mother based on someone you know?

> *Love,*
> *Mary Grace Ahart*
> *Salome, Arizona*

Dear Mary,

Susan Briarly isn't really based on any one person. I started thinking about old hippies—

such as Susan— where they might be now, what they might be doing, and her character came to mind. Hey, I'm curious, do you think Susan and Carson should stay together? Should Sam try to make peace with Carson? Let me know!

Best,
Cherie

Dear Cherie,

I know this may be a dumb question, but how do you pronounce your first name? I mean is the "ch" pronounced as in chocolate or as in shock? I've always wondered! Oh yeah, I love your books!

Sincerely,
Ebony Lindsley
Temple Hills, Maryland

Dear Ebony,

It's definitely pronounced like shock, and the accent is on the first syllable, the same as if it was spelled Sherry. Actually, Cherie is a nickname my parents gave me. My actual for-real name on my birth certificate is Sharon. But if someone called me Sharon, I wouldn't even know they were talking to me!

Best,
Cherie-Sherry And Definitely Not Sharon!